AF398494

OSITA OBI

The Monster Comes To Ceuta and Other Migrant Short Stories

novum pro

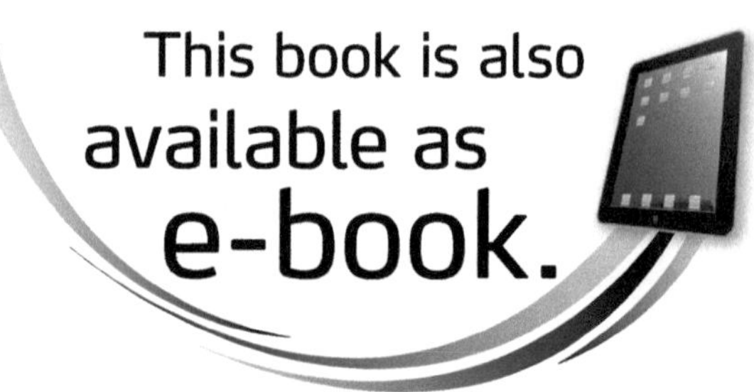

www.novum-publishing.co.uk

All rights of distribution, including via film, radio, and television, photomechanical reproduction, audio storage media, electronic data storage media, and the reprinting of portions of text, are reserved.

Printed in the European Union on environmentally friendly, chlorine- and acid-free paper.

© 2023 novum publishing

ISBN 978-3-99131-734-0
Editing: Charlotte Middleton
Cover photos: Vladimir A, Kazmulka, Andrey Popov | Dreamstime.com
Cover design, layout & typesetting: novum publishing

www.novum-publishing.co.uk

Contents

Billy stood in the shade arguing with the old man about something none of us understood. The moon was bright overhead. It was not a full moon, but it was bright enough to cast dark and scary shadows everywhere and to make us feel exposed. We could see the stars, bright and cool in the infinite expanse of the cloudless sky. The dark and hideous hills were etched inartistically against the greyish horizon alongside the silhouettes of hunched, wind-bent trees and craggy rocks. The surrounding scenery was of waste and wild – of boulders of rocks, towering trees and high-rising cliffs that made us feel so thoroughly inferior, insignificant and powerless. The damp and cool night breeze moaned from behind the adjacent hill, starting off blunt echoes from the ravines, valleys, caves, twists, bends and from the branches of trees and blades of grass. Now and then, a night bird flapped noiselessly across the silvery face of the moon. A cricket shrieked behind or around our feet. We heard a slimy motion, indistinct amongst the dark and stony undergrowth like some reptile slicing through clumps of grass. But we stood, chilled to the bones, not knowing any safer spot to put our feet on. Our eyes rolled and searched the dark and the damp undergrowth. Our ears were strained and painfully set. Our nostrils were dilated as the nauseating perfume of dust and crushed herbs played around the tips of our noses. We dared not sneeze or cough. We were warned strictly against any such mistakes. We could only scratch our noses to hold the tickling sensation in check.

The eight of us were huddled up at the foot of a small hill, near the crevice of a large boulder of rock. We were silent and trembling, more out of apprehension than out of the cold that later came with the breeze. The old-model Mercedes car that brought us here, its headlamps like the eyes of a grasshopper, was parked deftly beside a cluster of grass so that you saw only a little of its back fenders. The driver was still inside, waiting to take Billy back when the old man must have started taking us into the hills to Ceuta. That driver, I dare say, was a daredevil. He had given us not only the most frightening, but also the roughest, ride of our lives. And how he managed to cram us all into that car confounded us; the eight of us – Sandra, Tonia, Dolly, Chibuzo, Suzzie, Jerry, Osaro and myself. Jerry and Osaro were in the boot of the car, but that didn't leave any more space, considering that Suzzie was pregnant and that only the driver, his friend and Billy sat in the front seat. Well, that wasn't even the most confounding thing...

Why was Billy taking so much time arguing with the old man? We were getting more restless. From where we stood we could see the old man pointing at the moon and pointing at his wrist, indicating probably that he worked with time and that we had delayed. The tension in the atmosphere there was easily felt by every one of us. It seemed the old crosser wasn't going to be persuaded. We could even hear his voice, tight and angry, from the distance. And we could see Billy, too, gesticulating feverishly and matching the old man's antics in every respect. Was Billy withholding some money, or what? Why didn't he pay the old man outright and get us out of here? None of us could afford a situation where the old man would accept this crossing half-heartedly only to bring us to disaster. After all, we had paid heavily for this man's services. Six hundred dollars per head couldn't be called chicken feed in any country. I heard that Jerry and Chibuzo paid only five hundred each, but Osaro and Suzzie paid almost seven hundred each (perhaps for the extra risk Suzzie's pregnancy portended). My case was different from the beginning, although Billy tried to resist it. But I gave him only three hundred – after all, he had been my lover and had always had it free with me since I met him in Tangier. Silly. Why did men prefer it when you made them pay for sex?

Now Billy started in our direction, while the crosser followed him closely. The crosser was short and bent at the shoulders and didn't at all fit into what I had expected of such a legend. The moment I came to Algiers I had heard about a certain old man, called Ediomwan, who, knowing the shortest and the safest route, crossed people through the heavily patrolled borders of Morocco and the Spanish enclave of Ceuta into the Calamocarro asylum camp. Others had said they heard about Ediomwan even while still beyond the desert town of Assamakka. It was said that all who had him as a guide eventually found their way to Europe. So it wasn't with little delight that we had looked forward to meeting him. Earlier in the day the prospect of meeting him had made us lightheaded, breathless and fulfilled. You couldn't quantify the chaotic flux of emotions that raged through us as Billy approached with the seasoned crosser behind him. It wasn't surprising either that, despite the cold and the gathering mist, I was sweating on my forehead and in my armpits. Was the man behind Billy the famed legendary fox of the North African hills? Was this he who was said to be responsible for the crossing of over seventy percent of the asylum seekers into Calamocarro? Was he truly the man called the Messiah of the Foggy Mountains? Was this the legend of the Moroccan waste? Or had he sent someone else on his behalf?

A streak of disbelief ripped through my mind. Why had I expected to see a man who was tall and huge, with powerful biceps and tints of white on a coarse, medium beard? Perhaps I had battled with the weakness associated with my being a woman and the fear of the interminable ranges of rocky mountains on our way and had thought of a Superman or a St Christopher who carried one across obstacles. A man with thunder in his voice, whose powerful vocals alone lifted one across rifts and ravines. A man who could take up one's defence at the threat of bandits and the border guards.

But Ediomwan the crosser was not a man like that. He fell far short of all my expectations. When he and Billy reached the spot where we were huddled up, restless like slaves awaiting a slave driver's orders, we instantly gathered round them. I stood close to the old crosser but shuddered too much to peer into his dark and aged face. And as I began to remember that he was even rumoured to possess metaphysical powers with which he bewitched the border guards, I withdrew slightly and altogether avoided any eye contact with him.

Anyway, it was difficult to see his eyes. Below the bundle of Arab headgear he wound round his head, it was only his long and crooked nose, on which the moon fell, that you saw. But above his nose, the gap left for the convenience of his sight – a gap that was dark and puzzling, like a mouse hole – gave you the uneasy feeling that something toothy and creepy lurked and waited to snap at you. His lips, his beard, (he must have had some beard) and his neck were all wrapped up inside the dark headgear. He had a small shepherd's bag hanging on his shoulder. Despite tying his bogus kaftan at the waist with a piece of cloth and folding its sleeves up to the upper arm, he wasn't dressed as if he bothered about his chances of escape in the event of a chase. This was strange, because even pregnant Suzzie, like everyone else, wore jeans and a tight-fitting blouse. Rather, he wore only a pair of canvas shoes, which were easily seen in the moonlight alongside his wooden staff.

Then Billy began to address us.

'Now,' he said, 'you must be made aware of these vital points so that you don't bungle your trip. First, you must bear in mind that the moment our man delivers you at the entrance to the camp, my commitment to you ceases. Right?' This was too business like, I thought. Was this really Billy, talking like a lawyer too eager to protect his legal fees from an unsatisfied client? His tone this night was really worrisome to me.

'Especially to the girls,' he continued. 'You must be strong by yourselves. And always, promptly do as the old man directs you. The responsibility for your success is directly on your shoulders now. Don't count on the boys, because as soon as you are in these hills and mountains it is everyone for himself or herself. And at all times stay close to one another and be sure not to break the link, because you could be lost in the dark, where you can't call for help. Of course, the border guards will be all too glad to rescue you, but you know what that means – not only to you but to others as well. And at all times your mouth must be shut, no blah-blah-blah along the way.'

The old crosser touched Billy's arm and droned fiercely in Arabic, like a masked ancestral spirit.

Quickly Billy turned to us and continued, 'The emphasis is that you must do whatever he tells you, even if the border guards are close by and are looking on. This is important. Then another vital issue: to avoid the stupidity of that girl whose photo was found by the Guardia Civil the morning they entered into the camp, you must tear up photos and documents now if you still have them. Chew them up and swallow them, 'cos you won't need them for anything afterwards.'

Silence.

Billy then took a deep breath, looked us up and down one after the other – his eyes did not settle on me for even a second longer – and said, 'Finally, phone me as soon as you wake up in Calamocarro in the morning. Safe journey.'

He turned and walked toward the old Mercedes car, while we looked on, speechless. The driver rolled the car noiselessly out of the grass, and Billy entered and closed the door quietly. And, without switching on its headlamps, the driver started the car and drove off. Soon, the noise of the engine dropped into a drone and then into a buzz that quickly fizzled into the solemn night.

Instantly, tears rushed to my eyes and my heart began to pound. Billy had not said an extra word of encouragement to me – not even a glance in my direction to show that I had slept with him for months. How callous and brutal are the ways of men. A feeling of abandonment creased my joints and ran like cracks all over my head. You must be careful, I warned myself, or others will notice what had happened. True. And the beast had told us to phone him. Who? Me? He'd never hear from me ever again! Callous men!

The tears rolled down, nevertheless. But I didn't want to be caught crying. I wiped my eyes dry. With what lay ahead, wouldn't it be stupid of me to let in further corrosive emotions to melt this final resolve? I had come a long way without Billy and I'd go a long way without him. A journey that had lasted for over eight months was bound to be peopled by characters like Billy. Hadn't I seen worse in Abidjan and Tamanrasset? Ah, wipe your eyes, I told myself. And that was what I did.

'...Cuatro, cinco y tu, aqui, aqui.' The old crosser was counting us with his wooden staff. He cleared his throat and continued, '...seis, eh, siete y ocho... Que? Por que? Dios mio! Embarazada? Embarazada?'

He was muttering and examining Suzzie. He was clearly alarmed, and what he meant by those words we couldn't tell. They were either Spanish or Arabic. Even Osaro, who claimed a little understanding of both languages, was at a loss. Yet everyone knew the cause of his outrage. Why hadn't Billy the beast told him, or given him the extra money that Osaro and Suzzie had paid? What if this man were to leave us here and walk away? Sure enough, he hadn't expected a pregnant woman as a passenger. And, as if he had read my thoughts, the old crosser turned away and railed in the dark, stomping his feet hard on the ground and swishing his staff through the air. When he was through, he came to us, shuddering and letting steam gush out of his nose. But we were relieved that he came to himself quickly enough.

'Quien es tu hombre?' he asked Suzzie, as calmly as he could. Suzzie pointed at Osaro. How did she understand that?

'C'est moi, Osaro,' Osaro said in French and stood out.

'Tu? Con ésta?' The old crosser pointed at Suzzie's stomach.

'Oui, si,' Osaro nodded.

'Vale.' The old crosser nodded too, seemingly pacified that someone was at least going to take charge of that. And saying something else to Osaro which neither we nor Osaro understood, he motioned us to follow him, muttering, 'Avance. Desde ahora es caliese y silencio. Caliese, silencio.'

We shuffled after him, apprehensive in our breaths and in our steps. The fear of the dark crept into my heart once again. This wooded side of the hill toward which he led us was so dark that it looked like an entrance into an evil forest, as if the paling moon did not shine on it. Walking blindly in a crooked line behind the old crosser and making frantic attempts not to break it, we soon disappeared into a hideous grove. The brightness we had enjoyed earlier was snuffed out by the absence of the moon and by the thick, matted foliage overhead. I felt a chill in my heart but kept on, reassured by the presence behind and in front of me.

And so we groped along until we came out on a short stretch of open field that was shut in on all sides by dark and clumsy hills. We could see in the hazy distance ahead the old man leading the trail but couldn't for all the world imagine on which side an outlet lay.

Then suddenly the old crosser stopped and bade us lie down on the ground. He walked some distance ahead, crawled in short bursts and stopped. He waited, stood up and pointed his staff in the air, brought it down, pointed it to the left, then to the right and stabbed it on the ground before him. Then he motioned us to advance. When we got to him he raised his staff and bade us walk beneath it, all the time keeping the staff pointed to the sky. As I passed beneath that staff, the fear I had felt earlier melted away in his protective presence. But walking passed him my heart went cold again at what I saw on the side toward which the old man faced.

There, two patrol jeeps were parked a few metres away, behind a great mass of rocks. A man was leaning on one of these jeeps while another, with his back toward us, stood looking into the dull sky, exactly in the direction in which that old crosser's staff pointed. Up in the sky I saw a shooting star swish through the air and vanish in a thin, colourful streak. And soon we were crawling on our hands and knees far away, toward the foot of an adjacent hill, my heart still beating wildly in my chest. Was this, I wondered, how the old crosser bewitched the border guards?

Right around the rocky track at the foot of this hill the old crosser led us, until we came to a clearing beside a dense mass of what looked like elephant grass. He counted us again and made signs that we should calm ourselves and wait for him. And quickly, he disappeared behind the misty haze of the grass beside us.

A blanket of darkness came over us soon afterwards, and I saw on looking up that an enormous mass of dark cloud sailed slowly, as if with difficulty, across the hilltops, obscuring what was left of the hidden moon. And from the side whence we came, a wide stretch of grey fog came unfurling and spreading toward us. I heard the sound of the breeze, whistling through the blades in the grass and rustling the dry leaves and twigs on the ground. The insects became festive and noisy, shrieking and chirping raucously as if tonight were the last hours of a mating season. This made the night more intimidating; we stood huddled up close to the clumps of grass, murmuring amongst ourselves in voices one could scarcely hear if one were a foot away. Our breaths were hot and steamy and if one listened hard enough, one heard his neighbour's heart hammering at the cage of his chest. Suzzie sat down on the undergrowth and breathed noisily through her mouth.

'I can't make it,' Suzzie muttered. 'I can't.'

Osaro knelt beside her, solemn and exhausted.

'Easy,' he said. 'Don't go on talking; try to catch your breath first, right? It will be all right. I'm sure we aren't far from Ceuta now. We aren't.'

'I know I can't. I can't continue. Go with them, Osas; you can come and take me later,' persisted Suzzie. The remoteness in her voice and the finality of its tone really made us panic.

'No, Suzzie, you can't say that,' Sandra chided her. 'How can we leave you here and go? And in such conditions?' Everyone else was silent, not knowing what to say. We had felt earlier that Suzzie was completely Osaro's responsibility, but that attitude had suddenly changed and I was fuming inside. How could any girl have allowed herself to be pregnant in these circumstances? Some girls are certainly nuts, I swore. I felt like letting a slap fly across her face. The bitch. Even before we left Tangier, the prospect of her imperilling this crossing was a constant concern. But now we could only cluster round her as if she were a queen bee and try to persuade her. We were so preoccupied with persuading her that we did not know when the old crosser crept upon us.

'Qué pasa?' he asked, circling us swiftly. And without waiting for an answer, he counted us again and motioned us to follow him.

As we rushed after him, leaving Osaro and Suzzie behind, Sandra, or whoever it was, stumbled on a stone and made some noise. The old crosser flew back from the front and gave her a knock on the head. And not a word of sympathy was uttered in the preceding silence. Then I turned and saw that Osaro and Suzzie had caught up with us. Osaro was carrying Suzzie in his arms in front of him. How else was one to carry a pregnant woman? Osaro was the strong, wiry type, but we hadn't climbed any real hills yet and I wondered how he would manage a steep one.

Nonetheless our tense procession continued along the side of another hill. We weren't taking the rocky cliffs straight on but went around at the sides so that it felt as though we were going up a spiral staircase. The old crosser certainly knew the terrain. And just at the point when we were in a sheet of stagnant fog and our legs were beginning to ache, we began a slow and trying descent to the bottom of the hill once more. Here the grasses were tall and thick and the earth was soft and in some places marshy as well. Then we heard the sound of running water and the solitary croaking of a frog. The smell of dung and goats' urine wafted pungently through the air, quickly erasing the freshness from the cool air we had enjoyed earlier at the hilltop.

Unperturbed, the old crosser swiftly walked to the end of our trail and, in the dark, began to count us again. Then he took us through a path that was covered by tall reeds that rubbed against our faces. Out again on a clearing, beside a low-running fence of reeds, we began to hear a thunderous splashing of water against the rocks. I was convinced now that we were very close to the sea and my heart leapt up and began to beat.

But then we continued through a patch of small bush, jumped down a boulder beside another gurgling brook and burst out onto a dirt road that, on both sides, ended in darkness. We crossed this road after the old crosser had surveyed it and went towards another hill in front of us. At the foot of this hill he stopped and pointed out a path.

'Arriba aqui, moreno, muchos morenos,' he said.

We did not understand him.

'Vamos,' he said. 'Aqui, Calamocarro, arriba.'

We looked up the path he had pointed out right to the top where it disappeared into a dense grove. From the way we stared at one another in the dark, I knew that I wasn't the only one who was panicked. It was unthinkable that anyone could be living on top of that hill. Besides, we were expecting to be brought into a city, not into a forest. We were stone-footed and lost in wondering. But perhaps, if we got to the top we could walk into the city on our own. Maybe that was what the old man meant.

'Vamos,' we heard the old man mutter behind us once more.

And we began to climb the hill. When we were midway up, dogs began to bark. This put a fresh fear in us and we halted and searched around us for signs of life. From the height we had already gained we saw balls of light through the swaying foliage. On the ground were plastic bags, cartons, cans and bottles of all shapes and sizes littering the hillside. There was a sharp and choking odour of decay curling around us, sometimes taking on the pungency of stale urine. And there were sneaky movements on the ground that frightened us, until we saw that they were made by dozens and dozens of rats. Yet, all the while, the barking of dogs intensified and we looked back to seek courage from our guide.

But he was gone. Vanished.

Left with no option, we began to trudge up the hill with our hands on the ground. In the lowering darkness, worsened by the matted foliage overhead, we felt relieved that the winding path to the top was still visible. We followed it in single file, totally disregarding the hysterical barking of dogs around us.

When at last we got to the top, we examined the scene that awaited us. It was a dark and gloomy campsite with a few lamp-posts strenuously pushing the darkness away. This was no doubt the refugee camp that we sought to enter. It was like a clearing carved out of the heart of a forest with its thick canopy untouched. There were no brick or cement houses but rather clusters of loathsome tents lumped together like a herd of resting camels chewing the cud and contemplating a tedious trek at sunrise.

Mysteriously, the dogs stopped barking and a deafening silence ensued. There was not a movement in sight other than the patter of rodents through the litter. We chose the nearest tin-shack contraption on the left and tiptoed toward it, two at a time. And nothing – no sound still – but the same staccato patter of rats led us through the many tree trunks that were standing like guards here and there. I followed closely behind Jerry, who led the way, my eyes darting about. Near the shack, past a couple of tables that leaned on broken legs, we saw a man bent over and engaged with his zippers. He started and stared at us on hearing our footfalls. I stopped while Jerry approached him.

'You're just coming?' He spoke to Jerry first.

'Yes. Please, is the...?' Jerry's voice was shaking with distrust.

'This way,' the man said and left what he was doing. 'How many of you?'

'About eight.'

'This way, and make it fast,' he said and took us to the tin-shack contraption. 'Sit anywhere in here, but don't stand. The camp guards walk around sometimes. Where are the others?'

'They are behind those trees, over there.'

'Go inside and sit down. I'll fetch them myself. You are now in Europe!' At the mention of Europe, a swirl of haziness came over my head and made me stagger. When it cleared, I walked behind Jerry into the enclosure in which the man had told us to make ourselves comfortable, picking my way through the human bodies wrapped up in blankets on the floor. There was a warm, offensive odour in the air, which I ignored. I sought out a small space in the corner and sat down. Resting my head on a water can, I began to revisit, in all its vividness, the eight-month journey that had brought me here. I did not know that I had dropped into a bottomless sleep until...

'Call the Guardia!' I heard a voice shout. 'No, no, call the secretary first. He will call the ambulance. Quick!'

The Guardia Civil? The name terrified me and I jumped up, wide awake. As I grew accustomed to the daylight that pricked my eyes, I heard a lot of fuss at the other end of the room. Near the door somebody was on the floor tossing and twisting, heaving, groaning and sighing and stretching like a worm dipped in salt.

'Hold her hand and don't let her roll over,' somebody said.

'Gentle, easy, easy. It'll be over soon. I hope this isn't trouble for her?' You could feel the panic in that voice. And it was Osaro's. I got up and saw Suzzie lying on the floor. Two girls and Sandra held her legs together while an elderly woman talked soothingly to her. In one moment she subsided, in the next she raved and ranted, groaned and twisted. I had never seen anything like this. And so the commotion continued, attracting other people who passed by.

Minutes later, the thin wail of a siren was heard. In seconds, it blossomed into a full-blown clamour and an ambulance appeared behind us. Its passengers were white men in white-and-red clothes, with bold Red Cross emblems on them. Working like ants, they hurriedly whisked Suzzie away into the ambulance. As Osaro stepped up to the rear of the ambulance, an invisible hand and voice pushed him back. He walked around and around, confused and shaken. And none of us slept after that.

We, Against the Mountains

It was a little past midnight and it was drizzling outside. It was cold, too, such that when you yawned, vapour came out of your mouth like smoke. The rain must have been pouring down heavily somewhere towards Agades because we could hear a distant drumming sound, as if a neighbouring hamlet were in the process of evacuation. This was the exact atmosphere we had waited for these past weeks and we were prepared for it. We were jittery but excited that this moment had come at last. The beads of sweat on our foreheads told you that. We knew it amongst ourselves even when we exchanged glances. The quarts of hot drinks we had taken earlier had not touched the fears in our hearts one bit. This we knew, too, but wouldn't dare voice it. The fears had lodged that deep because this was the third time for Lawrence and me. And for Chinedu, who was to lead this 'beating', this was going to be his fifth attempt. We just couldn't wait to begin.

Chinedu stood up from the edge of the six-spring bed and blew smoke into the air. He kicked his climber's bag and looked around the dingy hotel room.

'I hope I am not forgetting anything,' he said.

'You can come back later for it,' I said. 'You always have.'

'Yeah? You mean we can always come back for it?'

'You and Lawrence, perhaps?'

'No, Lawrence and this bag, perhaps,' he said and kicked his bag again. 'I am here for the last time, men. And you, you can take over my bed when you come back.'

I snapped my fingers at him. 'God forbid.'

'Why isn't this guy back yet?' Chinedu said, looking at his empty wrist for a watch that had never been there. 'I hope he hasn't gone after that girl again. Or hasn't it passed ten minutes yet?'

'Of course it has passed,' I said.

The door opened slightly and Lawrence stood in between it, looking out into the corridor. He was talking to somebody.

'No, you don't have to worry; he'll be here in thirty minutes. So, dress up and come. If he fails to show up this night, we'll go together to his house, because I'm worried myself,' he said.

'No, no, no. No smooth talking any more, Lawrence,' a woman's voice replied. 'If he doesn't deliver by tomorrow, I must get my money back immediately. Understood?'

The voice we had just heard was Linda's, and we began to panic!

'No problem at all,' said Lawrence. 'I'm expecting you in thirty minutes; if he doesn't come we'll go and meet him straight away.'

'All right, I'll be with you in a few minutes,' she said, and her footfalls began to withdraw.

Lawrence quietly entered and closed the door. 'We must leave immediately,' he muttered. 'This girl almost caught us red-handed. What a witch! She won't meet me here! Anybody who has money to refund can of course wait for her.'

Linda was the violent type. She was a Nigerian, an Ishan girl with a short, stocky body. She obviously had been through lots of harsh and inclement weather in this prostitution business and was always prepared for a showdown at the least notice. Therefore, nobody needed any further prodding. She wouldn't hesitate to bring in the Moroccan police, the army and the air force to have us busted. She was street smart too, so it was surprising how Lawrence managed to con her into giving out two hundred and fifty dollars for a connection fee, despite the fact that she had been stranded in Rabat for almost one year. Perhaps that was the Lord's doing, to let us have a little cash with which to embark on this crossing.

'I am getting the hell out of here,' Chinedu said and he took his bag, crushed his cigarette on the wall and walked to the door.

'If that girl meets Mustapha in the bar,' he shook his head, 'then everything is blown.'

We grabbed our bags immediately and made for the door. One after the other we tiptoed into the narrow corridor and slipped through the back door into the poorly lit street. It had stopped drizzling, but big drops of rain still hit our faces intermittently. As we burst out on the main street a thousand reflections from puddles and streetlamps flashed about like phantom mirrors. The sound of running water came from the underground sewage, along with the odour of dampness and decay. We hadn't gone sixty metres when dazzling car headlamps cut across the road from behind us. The harsh lights came with the laboured sound of a Jeep driven at a demonic speed. We ducked into a corner and waited for the car to zoom past. But we heard instead the tortuous screeching of tyres and the abrupt death of the engine. We crept out of the corner like lizards popping their heads out of a crevice. In front of the shabby hotel that we had just left were parked a truck and two vans, and some men with long guns and batons were jumping out of the back of the truck into the smoke their vehicles had just belched. And as the headlamp went off and the men charged into the hotel, we saw from their silhouettes that they were, in fact, policemen. We crept out of the corner and quickened our steps.

'Twice lucky, aren't we?' I mumbled as we hurried towards the next bend. 'An informant is at work, or some bastard has swindled an Arab again.'

'I don't even want to think about it. Let's get the hell out of here,' Chinedu said. 'I only hope we don't go barging into too many roadblocks tonight.'

'Remember I told you someone said he saw Ogboru in town and that he is trying a fast one on a building contractor? Maybe he has succeeded,' said Lawrence.

'Let's get the hell out of here,' Chinedu snorted, as if he were going to bite anyone who hesitated further.

We walked further into the poorly lit areas, right round the lanes and alleys typical of an Arab neighbourhood. It was like walking through a jigsaw puzzle, but we already knew this neighbourhood enough to know where every lane and alley led us.

Chinedu led the way, however. He was always a network of nerves, and muscles too. Barely five feet, with a small head on broad shoulders, he was thickset and very dark in complexion, so dark that if he hid in a shadow you wouldn't spot him from a few metres away, unless he opened his small eyes or bared his ivory-white teeth. He walked fast, talked fast and had a general tendency towards impatience – a trait which he said cost him his residence in Italy. He had lived there for eight years and was deported three years ago. He would readily tell you that he won a legal battle not to serve the ten-year sentence he was given. But he would never for the life of him tell you what it was he did that fetched him the prison term. His ingenuity and physical strength were phenomenal. And he had employed both in shoplifting, car theft, drug-running and as a pimp and a bouncer. He would tell you everything the second week you met him. He'd say it first in Italian and translate it for you immediately. He spoke fluent Italian, good French and a little Bambara. He had picked up Bambara in Mali, where he was stranded for two years and survived through a passport transplanting syndicate. Although a Nigerian, he travelled with a Malian passport and would readily proclaim, 'Je suis de Mali; cent percent de Bambara.' He was a nice guy too, always with lots of stories to tell. It was in a deportation cell in Arfe that I first met him.

Wow! The dogs were barking viciously at the junction of the little mosque towards where we were headed. We quickly made a detour into a narrow lane. We passed a few stragglers who in flowing gowns sailed like ghosts. It was surprising that we hadn't met many people on the streets. Perhaps the drizzle and the cold had driven them behind the walls. Then we saw two men staggering towards us. And as they approached, we observed that one was in fact propping the other up. Because we were dressed in flowing gowns, the colleague of the staggering fellow must have thought that we were muslims, and he began to address him as we came closer.

'This illness has become frequent, and you'll have to stay in bed when we get home.'

'You are the sick one, Ahmed-hic-sick like a door mat-hic-like a-hic-take some gin and feel as-hic-great,' replied his friend, who quickly muffled the other up with his palm. As we deciphered the Arabic he spoke, we broke into laughter. The poor fellow was drunk and the ploy to pass him off as sober, but sick, had failed.

'Hypocrites,' Lawrence said. 'They are drunkards as you see them so, all of them. If he gets home now, he will fuck his sister. Pigs! Don't eat this, don't eat that, don't look, don't kiss, don't fuck, don't smoke. They do all sorts of dirty things behind those high walls they enclose themselves in.'

'But I'm surprised how they could dare, knowing what some religious zealot could do to them in the name of their religion,' I said.

'Even the zealot himself,' said Chinedu. 'What else would they do? I can't imagine any of them brought up in his home country not being a deviant of some sort. That's why when they leave their country, to get them to go back is like a life sentence. They'd rather die than be deported.'

'What a people!' I exclaimed.

'Weren't you there two days ago in the bar when that fat one that visits Mustapha bought us drinks? Weren't you there, Larry?'

'No, I wasn't,' I said.

'We thought he wanted Sandra, but he went chasing Chinedu.'

'God'll punish you, Osagie,' Chinedu cried.

'Is it a lie?'

'Who asked you?'

Lawrence and I burst out laughing.

'Why are you guys laughing like camels?' Chinedu chided us.

Thereafter we walked again in silence, with the dogs now barking at a distance. It soon started to drizzle once more in fine showers that fell like dust from the sky. But the cold had lost the edge to its sharpness, which was not unusual in this unpredictable Mediterranean climate. We passed a mosque and a big grocery shop and cut through Rue de Hamza. An odour of burning coal hung heavy in the air, commingled with an exotic smell of some oriental incense. Lawrence suppressed a cough, while Chinedu held his nose. With only two more alleys before our destination, I looked at my watch with the light of a distant lamppost. We quickened our steps, hoping that Ibrahima Dodi would be expecting us by now. But it was difficult to trust these transporters; they could disappoint you at the last minute. We had paid half the fee for him and his friends to take us to the outskirts from where we would begin our journey through the mountains. As we approached his house our premonitions grew. What if he wasn't there? A little hike in fare by someone else could easily bring us a disappointment. What if he wasn't there?

When we got to his house a heavy darkness hung round it like black fog. Chinedu said it was a sign that he was expecting us. So we followed him to the side window, where he tapped twice on the iron protector. And instantly the room burst into a flood of yellow light. Then we heard the sounds of shuffling feet and clinking metal, which were eventually swallowed up by the grating noise of a metal gate. We went immediately to the front gate to meet him, but it was another man that beckoned us to come in. Chinedu recognised him though, so we entered. Inside the compound was another man sitting on one of the motorcycles parked beside the wall. And while we exchanged greetings, Ibrahima came out of the house, quickly locked the door and asked us over to the motorbikes. We took our positions behind the riders who, my God, reeked of alcohol and cigarettes.

And off we zoomed into the night at a speed that got the engines roaring like demons. We literally flew along the roads, taking on bends and potholes at the same speed. The wind was hard and peppery on our faces. We could hardly breathe or open our eyes. We clung fast to the riders because it was difficult to tell when we would bump into another pothole. At first it was the interminable row of houses, stragglers, street palms and flowers that flew by us. But as we left the built-up neighbourhood, riding most of the time without light or simply with dimmed headlamps, endless acres of dark woods and heaps of rocks by the roadside shot past as if we travelled through time. On some occasions, we took dirt roads to skirt round checkpoints only to burst out again like frenzied riders onto the pothole-ridden asphalt. By the time we rode into a derelict construction site a few metres off the asphalt and stopped, my hands and buttocks ached and my head swooned. We got off the bikes and paid Ibrahima the outstanding balance, which he counted and examined with the aid of the blinking trafficators.

'Good luck, guys,' he said, satisfied. 'And remember to avoid the Big Tunnel. It's heavily guarded now. The woods by the left are your best bet. May Allah guide you.'

So saying, he and his friends turned their motorbikes towards the road, switched on their headlamps and shot off like rockets into the twilight zone. And like a monster impatiently awaiting its chance, the enveloping darkness rushed at us, baring black fangs and crooked claws. I had never felt so frightened and abandoned. It was like being trapped in the middle of nowhere. Like being caught up in a sudden break in circuit. Suddenly nothing existed any more. You heard no sound, smelled nothing, felt nothing and saw nothing. And suddenly there was a reversal, and all your senses woke up again and came to you in one mad rush – in boulders of darkness, in tremors wracking through your soul, in pungent smells pummelling your nostrils and in the shrieking and chirping of a million insects. It seemed akin to the initial fits of madness. You staggered and convinced yourself that all was real, that you existed and that you had come a long way for just this one goal.

'Lawrence,' I whispered, frightened and hoping that they hadn't left me in my temporary stupor.

'Yes?'

'Where is Chinedu?'

'Who? Me?' Chinedu spoke beside me. 'If you should go on at this rate, I bet you'd get lost along the way. Now, let's get our bearings right and get the hell out of this place. Tear away those gowns and hide them behind some rocks, fast.'

Quickly we tore off the kaftans and hid them, took our head masks from our bags and put them on. It was now the time to confront the mountains once again and we were prepared as best as we could be. Each of us wore two pair of jeans trousers, two T-shirts and a dark-coloured jacket on top. You couldn't afford extra clothes because you had to travel light. The bags on our backs were small, not even big enough for the bread, fried flour balls, water, biscuits, sweets and chewing gum we would need along the rough terrains of those ranges of cold and rocky mountains towering in the dark. We knew still that there was no way we could ever be prepared enough for everything; a lot still had to depend on luck.

We adjusted our masks and checked our boots to ensure that no loose lace dangled. Lawrence brought out a small bottle of dry gin and we took turns at it. It was warm and soothing as it burned down our throats. Then Lawrence dropped the bottle noisily on the ground.

'What? You don't know that that bottle could give us out even after we have gone?' I said.

'It's good that it happened now,' Chinedu said. 'We can't afford not to cover our tracks. No chewing gum or sweet wrappers; a lot of people have been caught for things like that. We must have time to hide them as we have hidden those kaftans. That apart, now let's see how we move from here. From here to the border is about three or even four hours' trek. We know that. But nobody risks it. And if we decide to break through here straight north, we'd get to Ceuta... about six or seven in the morning. But chances are that there will be trouble because of the many military camps along the way. So, like I've said before, it is better we go a long way to the west first, then beat through the north-west of Ceuta, by the ranges of the mountain called The Dead Woman. Then we'd come out by the other side of the border. This would take us more than a day, because we won't trek in the day. The said Big Tunnel is on the other side of the road we've just left, exactly where Dauda and his group were caught and deported, while the girls were taken away as trophies for the border guards. Now, let's get going.'

To kill our initial fears, we made jokes and laughed in very low voices until we came to the foot of the hill. But the darkness that met us there was so constricting that our voices dried within us. It was as if we had stepped over a threshold to a bottomless pit. You saw light, faint light, only when you looked up at the sky. And the silence that swallowed us up made our ears reel with the shrieking of millions of insects. A soft smell of burnt herbs lingered in the air ominously and seemed to thicken as we picked our way farther in, towards an indistinct path.

Then suddenly Chinedu said, 'Perhaps none of you have gone through this road before. This road is treacherous. It is loose and limey and the soil is slippery when it is wet. A little slip has sent many to the very bottom with severe bruises and a grating noise. You better watch it. Place your feet exactly where I place mine and there will be nothing to fear. Larry, I'm emphasising this because of you, not for Lawrence, who has carried out a series of robbery operations along the Benin–Onitsha expressway. He has always coped well in the dark, even on rougher terrains.'

Lawrence put his hand over his mouth to suppress laughter. Me, too.

'If these jokes don't give us out,' I said, 'nothing will.'

'It's a free world,' replied Chinedu. 'Go right ahead and laugh. This could well be the last joke for a day or two. The moment we get to the other side, no jokes, no talking, no breathing, only signs. Now, let's get moving.'

He still led the way. Lawrence followed. And I noticed in Lawrence's reflex, even in the dark, the fact that he shirked being at the back. But I kept this to myself, wondering that we hadn't even reached the dangerous regions yet and he had already begun to exhibit treacherous tendencies.

But if you knew Lawrence it wasn't something you couldn't expect from him. He was a good fellow though, as fellowship would allow, quite sociable and likeable; he always wore a smile on his boyish face. He was tall, slim and had a gait that seemed always on the alert. But he was thoroughly uncouth. He wasn't the type that talked much, but he'd talk with his mouth full and cared less if crumbs flew from his mouth and hit your face. And the many scars on his head and body easily told you the type of life he lived. When Chinedu said he was used to rougher terrains, we knew it was true. But it wasn't until I met him in Algiers that I learnt he was the escapee member of a five-man gang that robbed luxury buses and cars along the Benin–Onitsha expressway back home in Nigeria. When his gang was smashed and Lawrence declared wanted, the national dailies, even the national television, aired the news then.

That was two years ago. But now, he would readily tell you he was framed. But those we had met along the way who knew him in Uselu Street in Benin city where he grew up said he took to such a life when he was merely thirteen. He had a particularly bad scar by the edge of his left eye, where the Moroccan border guards had pummelled him with the butts of submachine guns as he'd tried crossing beneath border wires to Melilla. He had since vowed never to take on the Melilla route again, especially since he had, six months after, lost the ability to maintain an erection. And for somebody who was obsessed with the female species it was a living nightmare. An ordeal, to be precise. He hadn't had it examined yet; he counted on getting to Europe first and would use painkillers to douse the pain it often triggered.

I often sympathised with him, because he was a guy who would share anything with you, even his women. Even as we laboured through the dark, up this rocky hill, I felt my back pockets for the Nigerian passport he gave me in Cana after the failed crossing to Melilla. He hadn't charged me a farthing for it and I did not know any guy who could have done a thing like that without a fee. He had only said 'Pay me back in Italy?' for that was his desired destination. He liked the 'trolley'[1] business because it meant women and more women. And Italy was the European capital where his townsmen and women presided over the business. Even his sister and two cousins – prostitutes in Torino – were doing well, sending cars and dollars back home. Lawrence always talked about pleasing women and later exploiting them. And from the way he manipulated girls, especially that Linda, I had no doubt that he was going to do well when he got to Italy.

---

1 Trolley: a trafficker in women whose duty it is to deliver a would-be prostitute to a desired destination. They are men paid by the matrons of the business who themselves are often ex-prostitutes.

Suddenly I slipped and half-screamed!

'Ssh,' Chinedu scolded. 'What is it?'

'God, I don't know what happened,' I muttered. I was flat on my belly and my nails were deep into the roots of some shrub. Dust swirled all over my face and I heard the sound of rocks hurtling to the bottom of the hill. Lawrence held me by the wrist and helped me onto my feet.

'Your mind must have been somewhere else,' Chinedu said.

I felt a sharp twang of anger towards him, the sort of anger you felt when someone revealed an intimate truth about you. Ignoring him though, I busied myself beating the dust off my clothes while we walked in silence.

Breathing was difficult now, although we had barely ascended half the height. Perhaps we had taken it on pretty fast. And now, from where we stood we could see some settlements, not far off, brimming with dots of light. And a little farther away, a town stretched south, west and east, burning bright in the dark like a fairyland. The clouds sailed low overhead at an unusual speed, and I suddenly realised that the drizzle hadn't reached here at all.

We continued our slow and tedious ascent until we got to the spot which seemed to have been excavated. We walked the length of it toward the side where there were trees to hold onto. This made the climbing easier until we got to the top and sat down to rest and to relish the cold breeze licking up our dripping sweat. How tremendous was the feeling heights woke up in you and made you creative. As we sat there in those brief moments, watching the earth splayed out magnificently beyond us, I saw night as a beautiful and vicious woman, flamboyantly dressed in glittering and transparent apparel and beckoning us from the distance like an enchantress. I didn't know how I came about such an allusion, but it frightened me so much that I pursued it no further.

'We better get going?' I said and stood up.

No one objected and Chinedu took the lead again and began the descent. It was like going into a subterranean dungeon without even a candle light. All the time it got darker and darker and we stumbled more and more on stones, on hardy shrubs and on mounds of loose earth. The trees to hold onto were few and far between and some areas of descent so frighteningly steep that we had to sit on our buttocks and crawl down to where we could stand up again. Often we did this one after the other so as to check a fall by any of us. We kept on like this until we got to the bottom, where there were trees and rocks which made movement more difficult. Sometimes someone fell into a ditch and the others pulled him out, or someone ran into a stump of tree where only short and stubborn grasses grew.

'Let's see the time,' Chinedu said and brought out a pocket torch.

I came closer and we circled around it to prevent any ray of light from escaping. Through a pinhead hole in his clenched fist he shot the light on the face of my watch. It was a quarter to three.

'Maybe by four we'll be close to beating through the first of this chain of mountains. Let's get to that other hill first and check our bearing from the top,' Chinedu said, making it sound so easy.

And so we began. We did not stop or talk for the next forty minutes or more. By now I was surprised by how well our eyes had adapted to the darkness, for we no longer slipped, fell or stumbled into obstacles as before. We walked through the shrubbery and what felt like thistles, through clumps of grasses brandishing saw-like blades and through a colony of hardy trees. Occasionally insects chirped and we heard them fly blindly through the wind. Sometimes night birds shrieked and flew from one tree branch to another as we approached them. And by our feet we noticed sometimes that we had frightened a rodent or a reptile and we heard it scuttle across the undergrowth, rattle the twigs or slice through the grass and was gone.

Walking in silence with our minds tempestuous as we went, I knew that as I weighed and balanced my thoughts, and that as I revisited the vicissitudes of life that had put me on this perilous journey thousands of kilometres away from those that I knew and loved, that Chinedu and Lawrence had obviously chosen a similar path of thought. If we hadn't had mediocres, dimwits, criminals and kleptomaniacs running and ruining our political and economic lives, I wondered, what, with a university degree, would I be doing in this North African wasteland? It had been eight months since I had left Lagos, and God knew how my aged parents were faring. What if any of them was sick? What if anyone was dead in the family? How were friends Kevin and Nnamdi? Had those military tyrants put them on trial or simply shot them for the news they reported? Wasn't I lucky not to have been in the newsroom the day they struck? They certainly wouldn't have cared if I were merely a proof-reader or not. It was an atmosphere of blood and carnage as would have been left by some hoodlums. And they had gone ahead and set the editorial department on fire. In broad daylight!

You couldn't believe it had all happened in broad daylight to a such a prestigious media company. You couldn't believe that had even happened to you at the dawn of the twenty-first century. It was like the savagery you read about only in fiction and in history books. Or like the barbarism of such megalomaniac despots as Idi Amin, Papa Doc, Mobutu Sese Sekou, etcetera, which you read about in the dailies or saw clips of on the telly. But suddenly it began to happen in your own country. First, in the far and remote places, then suddenly very close to you: kidnappings, assassinations, press-gagging, arson by state secret agents, kangaroo courts, judicial murders, closure of educational institutions, currency devaluations, looting of public treasuries, collapse of financial institutions, draconian decrees, riots and an overwhelming increase in sycophancy and professional bootlicking.

It was incredible how a society could so quickly fall apart when military criminals and spineless politicians took over a country and exchanged morality for depravity. All the time you felt the noose got tighter and tighter around your neck, but you resolved to hold on. And then your friends began to disappear. And one day some state security personnel in unmarked cars came and set your workplace on fire and ordered everybody to leave the premises and never to return. You went home and stayed for months, hoping that things would change, but they never did. It got worse and worse instead, and your dependants got hungrier and more desperate. Suddenly you got a job again in another establishment and it seemed life would return to normal once more. But a few weeks after, you got fired because some secrets agents came and questioned the management about you. Yooop! The world tumbled over your head. Then you began a frantic search for a visa to Europe, to North America or to the Far Eastern countries. But before you knew that you could never get it, swindlers and conmen, colluding with some embassy staff, had duped you out of large chunks of your life savings, if not all of them.

Finally, you took the dreaded and lunatic decision to trek by yourself into twenty-first century slavery in Europe. And after months, perhaps years, you were still somewhere in North Africa, roaming in the wild, and in the darkness of the night groping through a maze of insidious perils like me, left at the mercy of wild beasts, robbers and ill-educated and sadistic border guards. And oftentimes you were in the company of illiterates, prostitutes and common criminals who understood only the desires of the flesh. Such became your lot as you quickly began to learn how to cheat and to lie in order to survive. And suddenly existence became everything, and morality counted for far less than when you'd left home. And after several betrayals and ordeals, you learnt too that in journeys like this only your thoughts were your true companion. You learnt to suspect and distrust everybody and everything. From country to country, you continually took lessons on racism and hatred. And even though you were a lamb before you left home you had to now walk about in wolf's clothing and learn to howl and bare your teeth. And as the days went and the kilometres passed you by, you observed with dismay that your values constantly rushed for the zero point. But you wouldn't think back any more because memories brought only sorrow and midnight tears. You only hoped that someday you could reverse the tide of these experiences back to innocence.

But you wouldn't dare think how you could really do that. You wouldn't because that involved a greater pain.

As we got closer to the foot of the hill the grasses thinned out. Above, the moon was now out but kept dipping into the cloud. I tried to look at my watch, but the shadows constantly spilled over it. I walked side by side with Lawrence, who presently was finding it difficult to keep the pace. Very soon, I hoped, he would have to take the rare position. I was deliberately stretching his pace. Suddenly Chinedu stopped and we rammed into him.

'Hold on,' he said, barring us with his hand.

Something immediately snorted by the grass in front of us. Then it growled and stirred the grass violently. We did not wait to see what it was. We turned and ran. We had gone metres away before Lawrence called us to stop, saying that whatever it was had taken off in the opposite direction. This incident really gave us the fright of our lives and my excited imagination ran amok. What if it were a lion? What if it were a hedgehog or a rhinoceros? What if it were a giant python? What if it were… I just couldn't put a stop to the flow of what-ifs that followed afterwards. Well, this incident brought the daylight to our eyes and woke us up to one more situation we had neither contemplated nor encountered in our previous attempts. Now, besides the inclement weather and the human dangers, possible attacks from wild beasts became a real threat.

We immediately changed our course. Veering over two hundred metres, we approached the hill from the western side. To get a foothold for an easier ascent here was difficult, because there were clumps of dry grass with thorns and barbs which clung fast to our feet and pricked so hard that we thought they had life in them. The stones beneath were equally hard and so sharp that we felt them directly on the soles of our boots. And long after we passed through them, the pain from the thorns and barbs went with us on the rigorous and slow ascent. When finally we got to the top, the fog was there amongst the woods, waiting for us. It was thick and woolly and swelled about us. We found a place by the root of an aged pine and sat down to rest and to smoke. We smoked freely because it was difficult to see the cigarettes a few metres way. That considered, we took our masks off and, in silence, gulped down mouthfuls of gin from a small bottle.

'I think we have to wait a little for the fog to clear,' Chinedu suggested.

'Wouldn't it give us better protection?' I asked.

'Protection, ke?' said Lawrence. 'It can work both ways. What if we walk into a military camp like Osawe and his group did, or have you forgotten?'

'Who is Osawe?'

'The guy that phoned us yesterday from Ceuta. They walked straight into a parade ground in a fog like this and he was the only person who escaped.'

'We won't make a mistake like that,' Chinedu said. 'When this mist clears a little, we can get our bearings right and move on.'

But the fog stayed late into the early hours of the morning. By the time visibility improved, cold had gone into our ribs and our legs were weary at the joints. But we got up, checked our bearing and left. It was just about after six, but it was still dark, because the moon had gone. The descent on this side of the hill was eas-ier, with solid rocks we could put our feet on and tree branches to hold onto. But sometimes, since time wasn't on our side, we jumped some metres down, from cliff to cliff, because we didn't want to go all the way up again to find some safer track to the bottom. We had contemplated this at the beginning and that was why we had avoided enlisting any woman for this 'beat-ing'. And, of course, Chinedu always reminded us that his first and third attempts failed because they had girls in their group who fell and let out such wild screams that by the time the men reached them, the border guards were already waiting for every-one in the valleys below. It was that risky.

Against our earlier judgment we hastened our steps to get to the mountain before it was daylight, having reasoned that spend-ing the day in the plains would expose us not only to the frontier guards but also to the bandits who patrolled these mountains.

Again, wild animals were more likely to roam the plains than the mountaintops. And since we would be sleeping for the greater part of the day, it was safer to secure a vantage point from where we could monitor our surroundings. So we were determined to get to the top at whatever cost and fast too, because the first half-lights of dawn were just breaking out on the horizon.

But we hadn't realised how fatigued we were until we got to the foot of the mountain. As we stood and surveyed its monstrous breadth we gasped, because we could not resolve from which angle to confront it. Its peak was hidden in the clouds and its jagged and rocky cliffs had enormous boulders that jutted out menacingly, as though they would hurtle down on us at the slightest puff of breath. We turned the way we had come from and marvelled that we had covered so much ground in so short a time. Then facing the mountain once more we looked at one another with question marks in our eyes. Could we really attempt this with the strength left in us? Or should we rest first and try later?

Silence.

'We better try,' I said. 'Even if it means getting halfway up and finding a place convenient enough for a nap.'

And that was what we did. We took the ascent head-on as if it were our final break. At last, we found a large boulder of rock that stuck out like a roof. We quickly tucked ourselves into positions beneath it, removed our masks, smoked cigarettes and slept.

I woke first. And it was as bright as if someone had come into where I slept, flicked on a one thousand-watt bulb and pulled away the blanket in which I had tucked myself. But I adapted soon enough and kept watch until Chinedu woke an hour later. We woke Lawrence up, chewed our fried flour balls and drank water. Together we smoked again, told stories and made jokes while we waited for night to come.

It was a long and sunny day, and we took time watching the mountainside for the slightest motion or intrusion amongst the trees and the grass below. At about four o'clock in the evening we saw, at the far end of the wind-swept plain, three men walking towards the hill from where we had come. They were white-skinned, dressed in mufti clothes and walked as if they were stalking an animal. We watched them until they grew small like dots in the hazy distance. We had no doubt in our minds that they were mountain robbers. And remembering the childhood stories of *The Thief of Baghdad* and *Ali Baba and the Forty Thieves*, I wondered why Arabs never really saw robbery as a despicable vice. The ancient Greeks must have seen a lot to have said, 'When you shake hands with an Arab count your fingers.'

We spent the rest of the day recounting our sexual exploits. How we used our black sisters to swindle or attract favours from sex-starved Arab men. How easy it was to make love to an Arab woman once you had cornered her in a situation where no one would ever find out. We talked too about how risky it was and how these sex-starved women would rub their voluptuous bodies all over you if you were stuck in a bus full of them. And if it was dark and the bus filled up, how someone would boldly wake up your penis, pressing against its hardness until she left the bus. We had never met a people so sexually holed-up and bursting at the seams. We talked a lot more on the issues and concluded that in this part of the world, religion and politics were man's harshest taskmasters, and that their women were the worst for it.

***

At last night came and we gathered ourselves together, put on our masks and left. It was another tedious trek and climbing. Sometimes we jumped from one projectile to another and over precipices and gullies many feet deep. We climbed a tree whose branches provided us an advantage to a higher elevation. We climbed, we trekked, we crawled and we slid on the ground as the challenges demanded. It wasn't always a clean ascent. Sometimes we slipped and rolled back to where we began, only to start again. Or we climbed to a pinnacle and, finding no thoroughfare, came down to search for an alternative track. And there was never a track except for the ones we were prepared to make. All this we did in the dark, with eyes shining bright like wild cats', until we got to the top, not the topmost of the crests, because those ones were still hidden in the misted sky. But we still felt the elation of being at the very top.

'Now, from here,' Chinedu said, breathless, 'straight across that other mountain is our destination. But we won't need any further climbing when we get there. We'll go it by the side until we get to the valley from where it joins another one that dips into the sea. And when we get down right now we must always stick together, because it is easier to get lost here. And the border guards could be anywhere around.'

'In which direction is Ceuta from there?' Lawrence asked. This question was suspect to me.

'Definitely by the right,' Chinedu answered. 'We'll see it from the top of that mountain when we get there. But we won't beat straight...'

'Why don't we get there first?' I cut in.

'We'd get there all right.'

'Then let's move it.'

'I'd suggest we smoke here first, if anyone cares for it. Lawrence, you'll need to, I know,' Chinedu said.

By the time we finished smoking, the fog had crept in on us once more and reduced the visibility. So we went along, lamenting the minutes we had lost. It must have been about an hour before we got to the bottom, with bruises and cuts on our hands and legs despite the double shirts and trousers we had on. And Lawrence now limped, having sprained his ankle.

Again, it took us hours before we got through the thickly wooded valley side and fought our way towards the curve that Chinedu had spoken about. We leapt across a lot of ditches, waddled through gurgling brooks and shallow pools of water, took the cliff of the curve with added determination and finally broke out on a farmland that stretched far into the distant mountainside. Relieved by this enchanting view of an open field, we advanced along its edge, towards the top of the highland, next to the mountain from where Chinedu said we could climb to the top and take a look at Ceuta. I had never been that close.

When we finally got to the top, excited and exhausted, we stood at its celestial height and stared at a distant pool of lights below, which under the moonlight glittered and twinkled like a dump yard of raw jewellery. Chinedu said that this magnificent sight was Ceuta. And that the impenetrable darkness beyond it was the Mediterranean Sea. Lawrence agreed. They said I could have seen the Rock of Gibraltar from here were it not for the fog. I hoped they were right, too.

We were tired and couldn't continue immediately, so we sought out a place on the stony ground and lay down to rest. We knew it was risky to lie down in a place like this. But we knew too that we couldn't catch our breath standing up or sitting down. We were so exhausted that we cared less if there were scorpions, tarantulas or snakes. And a little after we had settled down, Lawrence began to snore. He could sleep under any condition, this Lawrence.

'What time is it?' Chinedu asked me.

It was a quarter to four. Lawrence still snored.

'We better wake this guy up before he implicates us,' Chinedu said.

I tapped Lawrence's nose.

'Eh? Hmmm, what is it?' he said.

'Wake up, man, let's go,' I said.

'Me? Sleeping? I'm not sleeping-o.'

We chuckled at his distress. Some people were like that, you know.

We must have taken an hour or more to get down the other side of this height. From our experience so far, each ascent or descent was different from the one before it, and the next often proved more difficult and precarious. But on the whole, this lower arm of the mountain seemed to have taken the greater of our energy and ingenuity; even its descent was far more difficult than its ascent. But once more at its foot we took off towards Ceuta on the right. If we got clear of the plains before it was day, then God was on our side. We quickened our steps.

We came to a spot where there were many tall trees swaying noisily in the wind. And beneath was a scary hollowness that made spooky sounds as we stepped on the dry leaves. There were no plants and grass, only trunks of trees that made us feel there were border guards lurking behind each one of them.

Chinedu signalled us to halt.

'That hill over there is where I was caught,' he said. 'And beyond it is the border. But it is heavily patrolled, so we'll go straight instead from this point, counting more on luck, because I've never gone beyond its point. This is where we might need prayers.'

In the dark we chose only the difficult and the most unlikely terrain where we believed the border guards wouldn't dare patrol. Until we came up one small hill, we never reckoned how one such track would have led us into a military camp. The camp was poorly lit and had so few structures on the ground that Chinedu began to convince us to take a chance. But then a dog began to bark. And instantly a flood of searchlights burst into a sudden glare and swept over the entire camp, round and round, and we saw that the camp was not really as small as it had appeared. We turned away and descended by the other side of the hill, where we immediately began to search for the border fences. Chinedu hoped that we would succeed in no time. But just then we heard the sound of water rushing as if from a tap and stopped. This pouring out of water continued, and we couldn't imagine what it was. And just when Lawrence began to crawl towards it to investigate, we heard the soft pounding of boots and froze on the ground where we lay. Between the tufts of grass and where I lay, I thought I saw the shape of a man a few metres away, coming and coming, but it never seemed to be close enough, as if it were in a dream. Then the shape stopped and the splashing sound of water followed. Suddenly a silence surprised us when the sound stopped. And out of the darkness, out of the oppressive silence, a voice rose.

'No se donde esta.' It was plaintive and from a man.

'Perdido?' asked another.

'La luz, por favor.'

We did not understand what it was they talked about, but we were certain it had nothing to do with us. Chinedu said they must be searching for something. We hadn't gotten over it though when suddenly the headlamps of a car burst out full like fireballs in our direction and scoured the woods around us. Our breaths snapped and we waited for the worst. We saw the shape of a man drenched in light walk towards the edge of the bush. He searched the ground for something and walked back to the source of light. The lights went off afterwards, throwing us into a soothingly tactile darkness. We sighed with relief when we heard the door of the car slam shut. Silence, an oppressive wave of silence, rolled by. Then a match flared inside the car – a patrol Jeep – and simultaneously the engine came to life. The headlamps came on full again and the Jeep whirled round and drove into the road behind and was gone.

'Let's move it, fast,' Chinedu said. 'This must be the time for the change of guards.'

'I think so,' agreed Lawrence.

And swiftly we ran towards the direction the Jeep had gone. We met an asphalt road ahead, ran across it, and to our surprise we saw in the short distance, beyond an open stretch of land, a high wire fence stretching out on both sides into the darkness. We went for it, scuttling on all fours like soldiers going behind enemy lines. At the same time my mind was invaded by images of exploding landmines and bursting grenades, of sporadic gunshots and huge leaping flames. And above all these rose the grating cries of the dying and the wounded. My stomach began to burn.

But these images quickly faded as soon as we heard the rumbling of vehicles behind us. We lay flat on the ground and turned to see couples of harsh lights cutting through the darkness. One of the vehicles rammed into the clearing from which we had come and parked. The other one proceeded towards the main border post. But this was no relief for us. Men in the parked car came out and scoured the ground and the fence ahead with a powerful box of light. The light fell on us, lingered and swept away. Then it came again for several minutes, and we began to sweat. We lay trembling and apprehensive, not knowing what to expect next. And what a relief when it swept away again, and we sprang up on our knees and ran like wild hares to confront the wire fence.

In the dark the fence stood, looking impregnable and reinforced. And we had nothing with which to tackle it. This certainly was not how it looked from the pictures of it that we had seen, or we would have come with pliers. We did not despair, however, but attacked it immediately with our bare hands and teeth, pulling, tearing and biting at the wires, not minding that it tore and stung our flesh. There was nothing that will and desperation could not undo. Soon the wires began to snap, and I had enough gap to force in my head and an arm. As I fought through like a beast half-caught in a snare, the wires began to snap and to expand. And by circumstances I might never be able to explain I fell out on the other side of the fence and began to run.

I was surprised to see Chinedu running far ahead of me. We ran with the last of our strength, not looking back to see if Lawrence got through. By the time we stopped, it was because breathing was very difficult and we had come to a place of freshly tilled soil and rows of millet ridges. We dropped on our backs, not caring if anybody came to arrest us. The odour of dung in the air made breathing more difficult. And as for how long we stayed battling with our breaths I cannot remember, but we took off as soon as we heard a volley of gunshots too close for comfort, wishing that the guards weren't shooting at Lawrence.

the time we seemed to walk in a haze. My head ached, my veins throbbed and an intermittent flush of dizziness blurred my sight and made me stagger. This frequently gave me the feeling that I might not make the next hundred metres. But I always did and that surprised me. Finally we came to the foot of a hill that had looked so dark and monstrous from the distance that we knew it was covered with trees. By the time we began to climb it we observed that it had more rocks on it than we expected and that the cliff was very sharp. Luckily though, we got over it without incident and stood elated on its top with a feeling of triumph searing through us.

'That's the most difficult barrier that we've just gone through,' Chinedu said, breathing loudly. 'Patience is now the word, even if it takes us more days to get to Ceuta.'

I was too breathless to reply.

Silence.

'What's the time now?' he asked.

We looked at my watch together, then we sat down to rest, to smoke and to eat.

That was when I discovered that I was carrying on my back the shredded remains of my bag. It had been flapping after me and I hadn't noticed. Now there was nothing left in it, not a pin. As I removed the straps from my shoulders, I felt for the first time the cold stickiness of my palms. The blood from the cuts I had got at the wire fence had caked and my sweat was melting it. Yet I had felt no pain.

Chinedu's bag was not on his shoulders either. 'The thing almost got me stuck on that fence, so I tore the damned thing off and threw it away,' he said. 'Maybe that was what held Lawrence.'

'I hope they haven't taken him,' I said, expressing my fear.

'Me, too,' said Chinedu. 'But I can't imagine him allowing himself to be caught at this point, not Lawrence. God, not again. I bet he's got a dagger with which to stab himself. And he'd damn well do it, I bet you.'

'Kill himself?'

'Ha-a-ha! He attempted it before, somewhere in Marliwali or Nado, on our way to Melilla.'

'How?'

Chinedu first fumbled in his pocket for something and brought out a packet of cigarettes. We thanked God that he hadn't lost it. He lit one for himself and gave me the packet.

'How?' I asked again.

'When he was cornered after the others had been caught, he drew a dagger and stabbed himself in the chest and at the throat. That really frightened the Guardia Civil, and one of them, seeing the fountain of blood gushing out from him, pleaded with him, "Moreno, amigo, tranquilo! No pasa nada. Tranquilo moreno, tranquilo." But he stabbed himself again and again, ordering them to stop advancing. And when they stopped, he bolted, fast as lightning, leaving them more puzzled than before.'

'But how?' I was puzzled myself.

'How what? Do you think it was blood they saw? Ah, you should know it was a display of juju, now.'

So I agreed that I knew, even though I didn't understand.

And we stayed awake, chatting and getting suspicious of every whacking of the breeze against the trees and every ruffling of twigs on the ground. We waited in vain, too, for Lawrence to materialise from the surrounding bushes. But he never did. And soon we didn't know that we had slept until a staccato of gunshots woke us up. They came in sharp successive volleys and drove the sleep from our eyes.

'What was that?' Chinedu asked.

'I don't know; maybe we've strayed into the Algerian border,' I said.

'How could we? Maybe it's the military.'

'Which military?'

'Maybe they are training in the camp we just passed.'

'But they are far behind us.'

'Maybe it's another camp. They never get finished, you know. They're all over the place on this route.'

Still the sound of gunshots rattled on, punctuated by deafening explosions. We panicked, because it grew louder and seemed directed at us. We heard the sounds of unseen objects whistle through the air and through the treetops. We did not know where to run to. Just when we hid behind a stump of rock, something fell in front of Chinedu and I picked it up. It was a white slug – a rubber bullet! There was a training ground around and that meant we had to circumvent this route we had thought the safest. And painfully, we had to wait for another night, too. We spent a long, sunny day on the other side of the mountain without food and water. We smoked half the length of a cigarette at a time to ensure that we didn't run out. At sundown we became really thirsty and weak. Thirst makes you weak but hunger puts thoughts into your stomach. I began to think of the many failed attempts to get to Melilla and the long treks at night without food and water. I remembered how we picked bread from the refuse dumps and how some Arabs would readily give us some if they saw us. Sometimes we picked bread from pavements and from tree branches where it was deliberately put because Arabs hated the idea of throwing bread away. The bad Arab could rob or cheat you but wouldn't deny you a loaf of bread if he had it. The Arab woman was a gentle and a compassionate creature and would try to help if she could, but the fear of their men would always keep her miles from you. They were like that. I remembered, too, how we lived for weeks in a cave somewhere in the wilds of Marliwali and killed tortoises for food, and how we drank from a pond from which snakes, tortoises, birds and other animals drank. So going hungry for a day or two wouldn't mean much to me. But there was always something about hunger and thirst that made them such intolerable experiences. And that I could never understand.

But whatever that thing was, it made our day long and unbearable, too. When it was barely dark, we left westward to survey our tracks. We saw below us a settlement with what looked like two barracks at the outskirts. And we saw a dirt road like a pencil line winding behind it into the woods beside a hillside farm. And behind all these was a dark sea that faded into the northern sky.

***

When night came, we came down the mountain through the pencil-like dirt road, walking through the bushes beside it. Suddenly, gunshots rang out behind us and we took cover on the ground. On our left, a big security light came to life and swept across the hillside. A dog started to bark and its barking echoed through the many small valleys and hollows around. We stood up and continued until we came to a place of stones, of white and moss-ridden slabs and of tomb-like structures. It soon became apparent to us that we were in the middle of a graveyard. And not far ahead were the woods, at the end of which, we were convinced, was Ceuta. Traversing the burial ground, we took left through a grove of sweet-smelling plants and crept on the ground towards the woods ahead. At the point of entering the woods, Chinedu held me by the arm and pointed in front of us.

'What is that?' he whispered into my ear.

The object looked like the trunk of a tree chopped off at the middle, or more like the broken pillar of a derelict temple reclining on a heap of ruins. At one moment it seemed large; at another, small. I did not know what to make of it.

'I think it moved,' I said.

'It did,' Chinedu affirmed.

So we lay low on the ground and waited, our eyes fully fixed on it. Five minutes, ten, fifteen, and it moved again. We never panicked.

'What *is* that?' I muttered.

'I don't know.'

We waited in silence, breathing cautiously. Insects chirped shrilly. The wind blew, soft and cold. The scent of dust and herbs lingered in the air, damp and unpleasant. From the grass on which we lay, cold and refreshing dewdrops dripped on the naked parts of my face and arms. I felt ants scurrying all over my arms, but I did not stir. Nor did Chinedu. Then suddenly, out of the shadows in front of us, two human forms appeared and moved over to the pillar-like image we were watching. It stood up high and towered over them. It was a man! Surprising! The three of them left together and disappeared into the core of the darkness behind. In a few seconds we saw a flash of light. And what we saw puzzled us: the three sat inside a patrol Jeep parked deftly in the woods. The dreaded Guardia Civil! As the door of the Jeep slammed shut, the light went out.

We waited while they talked at length amongst themselves. At last, two of them left again and we rose and surveyed our surroundings for a long time. The big, lanky guard was still in the Jeep. On the right was a monstrous rock that seemed to reach into the clouds. On the far left, almost behind us, the security light still scoured the mountainside. The only option was for us to 'beat' from the tail of that Jeep. So we crawled further into the bush, cat-like and apprehensive, and skirted the Jeep in the dark and merged into the woods. 'Hosanna' was the song in our hearts! And we sang it long into the night.

Our nerves strumming uncontrollably, we went up a highland and came at last to the cliff overlooking the sea. The historical Mediterranean Sea! The sight of this deep, dark sea was the most pleasant I had seen in years. Balls of light floated weakly here and there on the top of it. I reasoned they must be ships or boats. Then we heard the protracted honking of a horn and the splashing of the waves along the shore. And along the edge of the shore a car sped dangerously with its headlamps full and dazzling. That meant there was a road down there and we rejoiced. We had been told how to locate the Calamocarro refugee camp and couldn't wait to get there. Only the night stood between us and our goal for now. It was just a matter of hours, and our troubles would be over forever. We could not sleep. We could not sit down and rest. We shared the remaining cigarette Chinedu had and waited impatiently for daylight to emerge.

When it came, we took the track down to the road below. From a corner out of the woods we saw Ceuta, bespangled with light, in the distance, and the lighthouse twinkling like a distant star. There, beneath a broad-stemmed tree festooned with wild creepers, we sat watching the road with fascination. Slick, state-of-the-art cars zoomed past, two Guardia Civil Jeeps and some racing bikes, too. The sea tumbled in waves while the many cargo ships and boats sailed on indifferently. Big white birds flew merrily about the shoreline, squeaking at the top of their voices. And suddenly, to our utmost amazement, out of this winding road came two black men carrying tins and buckets. We watched them seek out a place from a roadside parking lot. They sat down on a slab by the road and began to chat. We removed our masks and went down to meet them but on impulse stopped halfway down to check the plate numbers of the cars on the road. The letters were 'CE' and we concluded that it meant Ceuta. But just then a gigantic truck, engulfed in its own smoke, drove past us with all the letters of its owner, address and business interests written all over it. We smiled with glee and went to meet the two black men down by the roadside.

They were glad to see us. They gave us water to drink and, speaking in French, told us to quickly discard the tattered and dirty clothes we had on top. They told us to stay with them until they were ready to take us into the camp, which they said was no more than an arrow's distance. Chatting with them, we puzzled them with the tales of our valour, strength and fortune. Soon a sleek BMW sports car careened into the parking lot, and they left us and began to wash it. One of them said we had brought them luck this early morning and promised to take us to the camp immediately afterwards.

When the owner of the car paid them and drove away, they took us up a winding footpath across the road, through some woods and brought us face-to-face with the gate of the camp. Seeing that we were frightened despite our elation, they handed us their tins and buckets and told us to walk ahead of them and not to look at the two Guardia Civil who kept watch beside the camp gate.

As we passed the gate, my legs wobbled with delight and exhaustion. The sight in the camp was chaotic, yet the freedom it offered was enthralling. There were big blue tents everywhere and there were tin shacks in all corners. There were many people, blacks and Arabs, milling around in droves. And there were trees everywhere I looked. Trees and more trees, rustling and shifting in the wind.

One of our car-washer friends crept behind me and, taking the bucket from me, said, 'This is Europe. Look for your people from those rows of tents over there; that's the English-speaking section. We will meet you guys at lunchtime.'

Chinedu and I looked at one another and sighed profoundly. I made the sign of the cross and shook my head. Chinedu made the sign of the cross wrongly. And as my eyes caught his, the anxiety and despair bottled up in our chests for countless months ruptured into laughter.

The girl named Dolly

It was on a midnight in the last week of July that Jones sneaked into the camp in Calamocarro. The refugee camp was dull, misted and suffocating. And in the dreary morning that followed, Jones crawled out of the camp tent in which he was received and began to air himself in the mist and in the lazy rays that wafted through the heavily wooded camp. Wasting no time, too, Jones began to sniff at the backside of every girl that walked past his tent. The older tent mates observed this and, wasting no time, like Jones, suggested probable reasons for this he-goat attitude. Some said it was because he hadn't seen black girls in the past seven years that he had lived in Germany. Others who claimed to know him better said he was like that even in Germany. But one thing was certain: summer was in full blossom! There was the sun and the warm breeze. And there were the scanty, tight-fitting dresses the girls in camp wore which thrust out their breasts and tantalised Jones with the flagrant curves of their buttocks. The beach too was just down the road, where he ogled the semi-naked Moroccan and Spanish women who swam the sea in tights and bikinis. Life was simply astir and brim-full! And nothing thrilled Jones more than to gloat over those white female bodies as they emerged from the blue waters like ivory-white sea maids, with the water running through the curves of their buttocks and down their legs.

Voluptuous sights like that could upset many a man in many ways. So in his mind and in his groin, Jones grew restless. He grew aggressive and hostile too, on which account his tent mates suffered because he picked fights on flimsy issues. Yet no one cared to know that this sudden aggressiveness had something to do with the sexual tension searing through him. Making it still harder to know was the fact that Jones was notably loud and hypocritical, referring to the girls in camp as smelly-mouthed prostitutes who were on their way to Europe to make money.

His assertion was not disputable, but that he disdained having anything to do with them was contestable, for no sooner did he arrive in camp than it leaked out that he had in secret spoken to more than half a dozen of them. Little wonder then that in the weeks that followed, Jones went frequently to the beaches, kept more to himself and loudly vowed never to have anything to do with any of these smelly-mouthed, dirty-bottomed prostitutes. But he had reckoned without the cravings of his flesh and, most certainly, without the charms of a certain little Bini girl called Dolly.

It was one early morning in the second week of August that Dolly herself entered the camp. She was one of the eight girls and three boys the old veteran crosser brought in that morning. Theirs was the largest group the old man had ever crossed in one batch. That morning, as soon as Dolly's group crawled up the hillside and crept into the camp, their arrival caused a significant stir and rumour quickly spread around that a 'container' of girls had arrived safely at the port – the port being a particular camp tent taken over by the Bini trolleys who took care of the girls. Thus, no sooner was this rumour heard than the boys who had no girlfriends went nosing around the tent where the girls were dumped to catch a glimpse of them. These girls were mostly from Benin, Ishan, Agbor and the surrounding smaller towns of mid-western Nigeria. But because they all spoke the Bini language and had probably all lived in Benin City, they preferred to be called Binis, thus giving the Bini boys in camp an advantage over other suitors. But because the girls wanted money, not just love, they soon afterwards, one after another, went after the Ghanaians and the Igbo-speaking boys of Nigeria who did all the business in camp and would readily spend on any girl who smiled at them.

The Igbos and the Ghanaians in Calamocarro camp were like that. And this often angered the trolleys, who feared the influence of money on their girls and who for other reasons, too, preferred that these girls stayed with their tribe's boys, who understood the conditions for a brief relationship in camp and would not, like others, go about putting strange ideas of rebellion into the girls' heads. For often, there were cases of boys from other tribes and countries encouraging the girls to rebel in every possible manner, especially in resisting being smuggled into the Spanish mainland without migrant documents given in camp. Such legal documents put the trolleys and their madams at a serious disadvantage, because the girls could then challenge them, call on the police or run away.

The trolleys themselves were hardly in camp; they only visited. Yet this never loosened their stranglehold on their girls, whom they handed over to the caretakers, who were as vicious as the trolleys and would at the slightest challenge to their whims beat a girl into coma. And because the girls must be made submissive, the trolleys had no troubles taking sides – they always stood with the caretakers. Because of this, the caretaker had powers, too, that extended beyond caretaking. The caretaker suddenly became some sort of a tin god who must be appeased with privileges, too. It was, for example, the privilege of a caretaker to choose for himself whichever girl he liked and to give girls to friends and to any other guy in camp who did some business or other and was therefore in a position to buy him drinks or offer him money. And considering the abject condition of life in camp, the caretaker's position was enviable indeed.

It was this situation that made it least surprising that the guy who immediately got Dolly was a hunk of a guy from Ishan called Richie, who had a caretaker friend. And this Richie did nothing in camp but drink, smoke and drag his weight about. This not only frustrated Jones, but it angered him the more when he thought about the large sums of money attached to a successful delivery of a girl to a place of exploitation. A whopping sum of money from hips as small and obviously tender as Dolly's. 'These are a cursed people,' he spat and stamped his feet on the ground in quiet desperation. And gauging by the number of Bini girls he had seen or met in Austria, Holland, Belgium, Germany, Spain and Italy, he wondered if there were any more girls left in Benin and in the surrounding towns and villages.

They had all since vanished into the back streets and slums of European cities. What a people; what a culture! This Dolly ought to be in a secondary school now or, at worst, a housemaid in some quiet home in the country. But, no, here she was, already on her way to slavery. What a people!

Jones shifted his glasses and stared at two girls shuffling down from the road that led to the block dormitory called The Whitehouse. It occurred to him that he hadn't seen Dolly that day and he wondered if she hadn't been smuggled through the port to the mainland the night before. You saw a girl today and tomorrow you heard she had been smuggled into the Spanish mainland. Their lives were like that because their trolleys had to act fast before some mischievous lovers put some strange ideas into their heads.

Suddenly Jones felt a twang of shame. Why was he so bothered about this little Dolly's fate? After all, he was here entirely for his own troubles, which he had taken all the way from Austria through Germany to this place. He sure wouldn't have had anything to do with Spain if he had been lucky enough to have gotten a resident permit elsewhere. He sighed and quickly changed the track of his thought. But as two boys walked past him, staring and speechless, he recoiled, ashamed once more as if they had peered through the fortress of his mind. He looked in the direction of Dolly's tent and swallowed hard.

It was a Saturday morning. And it was unusually quiet. Jones could not see the sky when he looked up. An interminable veil of fog sailed silently across the treetops, giving him the uneasy feeling that the weight of the sky was, minute by minute, being eased on his shoulders. It was gloomy as far as he could see, and the thousands of eucalyptus trees that covered the camp only seemed to sharpen the cold that sailed with the fog. There was hardly any significant sign of life, because many people were still in bed. And the few that were out of bed walked clumsily from one clothesline to another, clipping damp clothes on the web-like lines around the tents. A little beyond Jones's tent was a tap that ran nonstop because its lock was broken.

And so the loudest noise Jones heard that morning was the sound of water rushing out of the tap and hitting the concrete slab below. He heard the twittering of sparrows, which were picking morsels from around the tents and from the refuse dump beside the running tap. A whiff of bad smell hit his nose and in turning to avoid it he saw the rats – big, clumsy and fearless creatures – scuttle through the refuse dump, shifting bottles, cans and cartons. To his surprise he saw two black cats sitting by the refuse dump, licking their paws and curling and uncurling their tail while lazily watching the rats from a distance. A little beyond the running tap three girls knelt by the concrete base of an electric pole washing their clothes grudgingly in silence. Then suddenly, a volley of gunshots rang out loudly from behind the surrounding mountain, rattling the vicinity like firecrackers. And Jones knew that if the fog was not there and if he stood up and looked through the spaces between the trees, he would see soldiers and their Jeeps looking like miniatures on that mountain behind the camp where they often trained.

Suddenly there was silence again. Jones looked about him and sighed. He was bored. Difficult as it was, he had to learn to adapt to boredom because for many months to come, from Monday to Sunday, boredom was the life he was going to live. He bit his lip and sighed again. It was going to be another dull day, he thought. And he needed no horoscope to contradict this reality.

In her tent Dolly lay tossing around in her sleep. Her face was contorted and her teeth were clenched. She was wrestling with the same nightmare that tormented her every night. With seventeen other girls cramped into the same tent there was scarcely any space within which to roll. She tossed right and left and she clawed the small mattress with all her strength and cried out, 'My toto, my toto-o! They are tearing me apart! Someone help! Help!'

The girl beside her woke up with a clouded face. 'What is wrong with this girl, eh? What is wrong with you?' she shouted. 'You won't ever let one get to the end of one's sleep. Na only you dey fuck for dream? Na only you? I say, na only you them dey fuck for dream?'

'Na Dolly again?' another girl growled from the corner of the dark and humid tent.

'Sandra, put on that light. I wan know why this girl no dey let person sleep efery night.'

The light came on and Dolly, now awake, turned away, embarrassed. Linda, the girl who had ordered the light to be switched on, went to Dolly where she lay. 'Now, my sister, I wan ask you,' she said, 'na who dey come fuck you every night like that? And you sef you no dey say "no". Toto dey scratch you no be small, eh? Na to quick-quick open your nyash you sabi and then to wake everybody up when they don begin bash you. Who dey come bash you like that? Abi na Richie?'

Dolly was silent. There was no way of letting anyone in on the tornado of pain that raged through her.

'Maybe na her water husband sef,' said Sandra.

'I wish I get husband like that who sabi im duty well,' Lizzy said.

'How long is his prick?' asked another girl sleepily.

'Maybe one foot-two,' replied yet another.

'That kind prick go scratch person toto well-well-o.'

'How una even know sef? Na Dolly tell una?' asked another girl from the furthest part of the tent. 'Abeg put off that light joo, make I sleep!'

By the time the light went off and darkness rushed back, Dolly thought about the nightmare that had always tormented her since she came into the camp. So much so that she dreaded the stealthy approach of every night. She dreaded having to think about it in the day and sometimes having to sleep.

It was like the sight of a bone-deep scar that opens a floodgate of bitter memories. And always it was the same faces, the same place, the same circumstances, the same nightmare. The faces were those of Arab mountain robbers, the place was the rocky waste of the Algerian frontier, the circumstances were the attempted crossings into the Melilla borderline and the nightmare was the gang rape she had suffered at the hands of those robbers. It had been five weeks since this incident took place, yet she lived through it every night in its excruciating details and in all its viciousness. God, she'd give anything to forget. But how does one forget? Dolly did not know. Even in the day it was difficult to get it out of her mind, especially in this camp, in this Ceuta. For there were lots of Arabs of Morocco and Algeria in camp, while the Centro itself milled with Arabs, the sight of whom immensely troubled her.

Dolly would take a diversion if she saw a group of Arabs ahead of her and would miss a bus if there weren't enough blacks in it. She hated the sight of long beards, turbans and flowing gowns and she desperately wished to be smuggled into the peninsula quickly, where she hoped the process of recovery would be easier on her way to Italy. For how long was she going to cope with this?

But she was a cheerful girl, Dolly was. And you wouldn't know that anything deeply troubled her. She was one person everyone knew had a ready smile. She was pretty and petite, with a soft, clear, small voice that made you think she wasn't anywhere near twenty. Her eyes were small and brown and her lips were full. She had lovely rings on her neck and gesticulated with a peculiar positioning of the head that made you nostalgic about your own years of innocence. She had toning marks on her cheeks, armpits and thighs, and on her left cheek was a faint tooth mark where a Moroccan client had bitten into her. On the small of her back and on her buttocks were several claw marks left too by over-excited clients in Tamanrasset and by the bandits of Melilla who abducted and raped her for days. Dolly's breasts were full and firm and surprisingly had no scars except for one left by a senior officer of the Moroccan police, who even video-ed one of their several sexual encounters. She was no more than four foot two but somehow managed to carry herself like a lady. She loved tight-fitting blouses, shorts and skirts because they highlighted her delicate features. And when Dolly smiled, glints of glamorous expectations shone in her eyes like algae-coated pearls awaiting discovery at the bottom of a clear, stagnant pool. Her entire life seemed to be made like that. A life of yet undiscovered gems, of unrealised expectations and of brittle dreams.

And Dolly had plenty of these dreams too, most of which were tailored by her passion for big things – big cars, big houses, jumbo jewellery, big men, costly clothes, expensive perfumes, shoes and bags and all the glittering and glamorous things that come in disproportionate sizes and prices. That was Dolly, only she hadn't realised her dreams yet. She often dreamt of shipping posh cars home for her own use and then several other cars for her parents.

And now her head reeled with too many things she dreamt to do: to build a plush duplex for her mum and the younger ones, to buy the best dresses, make-up, perfumes, jewellery, bags and shoes. And to befriend the rich and the powerful. She wouldn't like to be like her elder sister, Adesuwa, who disappointed her parents by marrying early without first paying for what it took to raise her. She would never be a disappointment like Adesuwa. God forbid! In fact, Auntie Julie of Ikpoba Hills was her idol. That lady was powerful and she swam in money. She had all there was and even more. Who did not know Auntie Julie in the whole of Benin City and beyond? Even musicians sang her praises and wouldn't release their albums unless a track was dedicated to her. She had hotels all over the city, even, some said, in Lagos. And all these hotels were filled with girls! And she had a successful 'girl-crossing' business from Nigeria to Italy and Belgium. It was said that every girl wished to work for Auntie Julie in Italy, and as such she didn't even know all her girls by face, let alone knowing them by their names. And to think that when she began, people referred to her as a common prostitute who could be had for a penny. And look at where she was! Who would dare say such nasty things now that she was the toast of the rich and the powerful in society? What was more, whenever in town, Auntie Julie moved in a convoy of no less than seven cars! What could be more than that? She was every mother's dream daughter. Ask any mother in Benin City today. Auntie Julie was.

But Dolly had other reasons, besides, why this trip to Italy excited her. It seemed everybody was in Italy shipping back cars and sending glittering things to family and friends. Even

Queen, the ugly Queendaline of the Ire-Ewu Street neighbourhood. Queen, the ugly duckling, was said to have sent a Toyota
Corolla to her mother within nine months. You couldn't believe it. That meant that finer girls would do better than that.
Nothing was more logical. The last time Dolly visited her village
from Lagos her mother had told her that three of her friends
had gone to Italy to hustle and that she and her father had succeeded in persuading the gentleman who helped Dolly's friends
to travel to help Dolly.

At this information Dolly was delighted beyond even her own
imagination, for she had twice tried getting this link by herself
but was often cheated out of it by smarter girls. Now was the
assurance that she wasn't ever going to be a disappointment to
her family. As for her friends who became swollen-headed because they got admitted into higher schools, they would be dis-
graced in a matter of months when she would send her first car
back home and stir the whole neighbourhood to envy. So sure
was she of that, Dolly visualised how the neighbours would be
swarming around the red car – Dolly liked red cars – she would
send to her mother and how the womenfolk would envy her
mother and wish they had a daughter like Dolly.

Such were her dreams, but that was at the beginning. The
dreams were still with Dolly, but the eight months of life on the
road and through the desert had reshaped them and made them
brittle. This morning, as she lay in bed and thought about her
life, Dolly couldn't quite decide whether this travel was going to
be worth the trouble after all. This for sure wasn't the way every
other girl travelled to Italy and told beautiful stories.

Eight whole months and two weeks on the road! Their trolley had deceived everybody, including her parents. The man
had promised to take her and three other girls by aeroplane to
Cote d'Ivoire, then to Morocco and from there straight to Italy,
where a certain matron eagerly awaited their arrival. The man
had shrewdly calculated the flight tickets, connection fees, passport and visa fees, etcetera, and had brought his price to forty-five thousand dollars. And Dolly's father and uncle had signed

using a portion of the family land as collateral, the huts and the cash crops therein included. Yet since Dolly began this travel, she hadn't known what a tarmac looked like, hadn't even seen an aeroplane except those anyone could tell were there by the white tracks they left far up above. On the contrary, the man had smuggled them through the precarious borders of West Africa from Benin Republic, through Togo to Ghana, Cote d'Ivoire, Mali, Algeria and finally to Morocco. And often he kept them in cheap backstreet hotels and disappeared for days, sometimes for weeks, without money for food, leaving them to canvass for men in order to survive. And whenever he reappeared he told well-laced stories of how the money he expected from Italy had not arrived.

Later, because he began to like Dolly and to sleep with her, he told her that the woman who had actually paid him to bring the girls was in Italy and that she had changed her mind about the routes and the flights and the visas and blah, blah, blah. This revelation made Dolly despondent even though he cared extra for her. And she couldn't think of having had even a split-second of happiness in her entire life whenever she sat and weighed the past against the present. It had been rough all through, very rough. She had been raped by anybody who felt he could get away with it. She had slept for days in cellars, hiding from the police. And the backstreet lodgings where she and the other girls stayed were frequented by rogues, drunks and robbers who often had other things on their minds than sex. You had to count on a lot of luck when dealing with them. Even when you had a fever or your period, you had to sleep with beggars – the lame, the blind and the deformed. You had no choice, or you starved. And every morning you woke up sick because your two-by-five-metre room where eight people slept had no windows, and the heat and the sweat and the breath produced such stench as made your lungs ache when you woke.

She turned her face to the other side of the mattress and sighed. She could hear some of her tent mates snoring, but that quickly faded away as her mind went back in time again.

Life in Tamanrasset was a little easier, Dolly thought, because the men there paid well for sex and would gently queue up when the police were not there.

Yet you easily got tired of living, because you didn't know where you were headed. Or whether it would ever be over, because in Cote d'Ivoire and in Mali she had met many girls who had been on the road for two years without any hope of ever getting to Europe any more or even going back home. And by the time three other girls joined Dolly's group from Ghana her worries tripled, even though the trolley had promised her that she would be in the first batch to be crossed into Ceuta. She had learnt to disbelieve and to distrust everything and everybody. So it was a complete surprise when one afternoon the trolley came back and told her and the other girls to get ready for a midnight crossing. And, miraculously, in less than eight hours they had found themselves here in Ceuta, crawling up the steep side of this Calamocarro camp thanks to a certain old guide called Ediomwan, who had skirted all those ranges of monstrous-looking mountains which had so mercilessly frightened them.

But here in Ceuta, nothing changed except that you didn't have to fuck in order to eat. There was the food donated by the Red Cross. And the men? You even had to choose who you wanted to go out with. There were even some refugees here who paid better for sex. But you had to be careful not to make it seem as if your choice of men was dictated by their money. Men didn't like it much if it seemed they were paying expressly for sex. You had to make them believe you liked them, so that they would be ready to pay more than they would have paid for straight sex. Since men were like that, you had to help them play along. You could choose, even here, to tell whomever desired you that you were a virgin. Men believe that, you know! They would even sympathise with you if you lied hard enough that you were ignorant of what you were here in Europe to do, that you were deceived that you were coming for a restaurant job. Pretence was easier here in camp and it was lovely to be able to pretend once again, something a girl could not do without, you know.

And although everything she saw fell short of her expectations, life in the camp was a lot better for Dolly. After all the thirst and the hunger, after all the humiliations and the inhuman lodgings, and after the endless agony of hopelessness, she could now sleep knowing that as sure as the sun would rise tomorrow, hope would never again be lost. Now she could even go to the camp clinic for a mere common cold and be attended to. Her second week in camp was such a relief, because she had gone and got treated for gonorrhoea, chlamydia and other sexually transmitted diseases, which the Red Cross clinic had diagnosed. And she didn't spend a farthing on the treatment. It was not only that which made her happy. That she wasn't pregnant in those horrendous months was in every sense a miracle. Because on the road the preventives were crude and unreliable – a combination of Andrews Liver Salts, hot drinks and potassium powder.

God, what a relief! Here in Calamocarro it was lovely to be human again and to be pampered by broad-shouldered men once more. And the boy Richie had awakened that tender portion of her heart that had been frozen for months. When now she listened to love songs, she sometimes felt the lyrics were written for her. That gave her life meaning. And above everything else Dolly liked the lust in men's eyes. Even last night, when she went to that other tent to buy biscuits and Coca-Cola and that clean-shaven guy, who always wore white glasses, patted her on the back and winked at her, she had felt such a sensation which she hadn't felt in a long time. That was the kind of guy she wanted: such broad shoulders, thick neck, bright eyes and a deep baritone voice that could coo any girl to sleep. And his skin was glossy and dark; he was unlike Richie, who was fair-complexioned and spoke with the voice of a woman. She preferred this guy, who it was said came from Austria. Not this Richie, who came penniless, from behind the mountains like herself. This guy from Austria had kind eyes and smelled of masculine love, unlike Richie with his shifty eyes, who always smoked hashish and got himself drunk. If that guy flirted with her again, she would accept him. Already he had asked her to help him buy a few things when next she went to town. Sure, she wouldn't forget. No girl forgets the solicitations of a guy like that. But why was it that he behaved shy the way he did? Dolly couldn't understand. Well, she had to wait and see, because there often was a reason behind the actions of men, especially those you thought were shy. What was that guy's name? Had she forgotten? No, how could she? Jones; yes, his name was Jones. He should have been called Peter, for there was something solid and macho in his physique.

And so it was that when Jones struck, no one knew. And how Dolly fell without even a thud became in itself a mystery in Calamocarro. And utterly mystified were those who did nothing in camp but poke their noses into affairs other than theirs. The beginning of their relationship was a mystery. Someone said after it began that it was like a wine-tapper's fart at the top of a palm tree that left inquisitive houseflies confused. What everybody in the camp felt was the stormy passion that went with their love affair. Jones, who formerly prayed often and went to church on Sundays, stopped altogether. Now he preferred to stay indoors and watch over the tent when everyone else was gone. His reason? To keep away those thieving Arabs in camp who often raided the tents when everyone had gone to church. But his tent mates, though grateful, knew it was a time to kiss and neck and wrestle with Dolly, who herself had forgotten everything about Richie and the blessings she often received from attending missas.

And in the days that followed, Dolly's laughter was heard in the afternoons and evenings ringing out ceaselessly from within Jones's tent. Jones forgot the beaches and the solitary walks and stayed indoors joking and laughing and carrying Dolly about the tent on his back. He became too engaged to be annoyed or distracted. Even when his tent mates gossiped about his age or reminded him what he had said about 'foul-mouthed, dirty-bottomed prostitutes', he waxed his ears and labelled them as envious. He played with no one else and he chatted with no one. If you ever saw him in company inside or outside the camp, it was in Dolly's. And soon the story went round that he was under a spell, and that Dolly, being a Bini girl, had had him bewitched. That perhaps was the only explanation anyone had as to why a thirty-eight-year-old man could have been so obsessed with a girl as small as Dolly. But Jones was indifferent to whatever anyone cared to think. He made sure Dolly left her tent to sleep with him every night, so that in the day and at night his bed creaked. This went on and for too long. And soon his tent mates began to complain. But Jones would have none of it; he was prepared like a man to protect the love he had found. Once, he even threatened and vowed in broad daylight that he was prepared to kill or be killed. And that sent the signal, because his tent mates, being cowards who saw no reason why they should contemplate death for a cause like that, quickly chose to ignore him. And so the fiery love affair rolled on sweetly, swiftly and undisturbed into the first week of October.

But Jones did not feel secure, however, because last weekend, Dolly's caretaker had, with the help of a hired crosser, tried to cross Dolly through the port to Algeciras but failed. Jones was nevertheless aware that Dolly's travel document was detected as fake, while Dolly back in camp lived the day not knowing whether to laugh or to cry. If the caretaker and the crosser hadn't openly mourned the three thousand dollars they would have shared there was no way Jones would have known. Consequently, as the next weekend approached, Jones became deeply disturbed. He wasn't going to let anybody take Dolly away like that. So on Wednesday he took Dolly to town and bought her a pair of shoes, two blouses, skirts and some pants. Dolly wanted a ring too. Jones said he hadn't enough money for the moment. But the truth was that he had reasoned that a ring would mean more than he wanted out of the relationship. All the same, Dolly was so excited that by the time Jones took her to a cheap hotel and paid for a room, her eyes were already dilating for the vigorous lovemaking she anticipated.

Soon enough Jones was on her and all over her as soon as they shut the door behind them. His big, strong muscles twitched and cracked in ecstasy all over her as he delved into her tender flesh in short, rapid thrusts while his strong and broad hands caressed her hair, her back and her excited breasts. God, it was so lovely to be filled up by a man who was every inch a man, and lovelier still to be swept away by that ravishing flood of pleasure that comes with the total submission to a manly love. Dolly's heart seemed suspended in a pleasant limitlessness. Then there was the heat and the sweat, the muffled screams and the laboured breath and there was the grinding and the pelvic rhythm that unravels the mystery of exploding white clouds. The lingering in limbo followed the soft descent from the floating clouds, then the serene moments of exhaustion.

Silence. A long silence.

Then Dolly turned toward the wall. How did a girl leave a guy like Jones? He could be so loving; he was so kind and he cared more than anyone she had ever met. How did a girl leave a guy like that? And knowing that she was probably sleeping with Jones for the last time, she began to sob. There was going to be another crossing tonight, but she was under an oath not to tell. And this time she feared it was not going to fail, because her caretaker had not only transplanted her passport photograph onto a genuine document but had found out the safest hour in which to do the crossing. Yet it was difficult not to tell Jones, so she sobbed louder.

'What's the matter?' Jones was quick to notice.

Dolly did not answer.

'Dolly,' he cooed into her ear. 'What's the matter?'

She hesitated, then, 'Nothing.'

'Nothing? You want me to believe that?' He turned her toward him and she buried her face in his hairy chest.

'Who would you tell if you don't tell me?' he persuaded her.

Silence.

'The problem is that I am not supposed to tell,' she said.

'Even me?'

'I took an oath.'

'What oath?'

'Not to tell.'

'Is it that woman? Did she phone you again?'

'No. But she will phone tonight.'

'Why? Give me her number; I will call her myself.'

'You won't talk to her,' Dolly persisted. 'Efosa would kill me.'

Jones knew the powers of Efosa, the caretaker, over a girl like Dolly, and his own powerlessness angered him. How could a spent old prostitute far away in Italy wield so much power over the life of a little girl she had never even met? He wasn't going to let that happen. And if that guy Efosa dared touch her, then that was all he needed to expose those pimps and trolleys in camp. But could he? He wished he had the nerve to expose them. Then he wished he had money enough to buy Dolly out himself. He had seen it done, even in camp here. Just a week ago a Bini man came from Holland, bought two girls and paid a crosser who took them into the peninsula for him. It didn't cost beyond thirteen thousand dollars per head. But to pay thirteen thousand dollars for a girl? If only he had that much. But what if he hadn't? Yes, but what if Jones hadn't? No one was going to take Dolly away like that. She had to get her papers first, he swore.

He shifted Dolly's head away from his chest and looked into her eyes.

'Listen,' he said. 'You don't have to go if you don't want to. You have that right here in Europe. Your madam can only make distant phone calls: she can't come. Efosa himself understands the risk of applying force. I am not saying that you won't eventually go to her. No. It's just for her to be a little more patient until you are posted with your documents. Did you tell her that in two weeks they will be posting out only women?'

'I did, but she wouldn't hear of it. She said she didn't spend her money bringing me here for Spanish papers. She wouldn't hear of it at all. She screamed and screamed until the phone fell from my hand,' Dolly explained.

'Do you know why?' Jones asked her, after a spate of silence.

Of course Dolly did not know.

'It's for the same reason I told you earlier. She knows that that paper is your right in Europe, and your life. With it you wouldn't depend on her or anybody else. You could do anything you want to do. Here in Europe, paper is existence; paper is everything. You won't live underground like I have done all these years. Almost seven years in Europe, and here I am, still here in a refugee camp, living in an animal tent and queuing up for food, just to get a legal document. I left off everything, every responsibility for the months I am going to spend here. I am not doing that for nothing. I know you won't understand, but I can't afford to see you make this terrible mistake. Do you know that you can't go to the police, to the bank or to the hospital without this paper? You'd need somebody who has this paper to be able to do anything. Worse is that you can't get a job. Or tell me, do you intend to do the job which that woman wants you to do?'

'No,' cried Dolly, 'she'd have to kill me first.'

'And kill you she will. Better think about it.'

Dolly thought about it for long and in silence, without understanding it though, while Jones snuggled close to her and cuddled her. Soon he began to kiss her passionately and Dolly withdrew from him.

'The consequences will be too much for me,' she muttered, staring blankly. 'Not only for me, but for my family. My father signed off the family land. They would attack my family; I've seen it all before. On my part, too, it would be suicidal because of the oath I took before the Uben River, before the very priestess. They took everything they wanted from my body, everything with which to make me mad – my hair, my nails, my pubic hair, my menstrual discharge and my pants. And I used my tongue to pick the kola nut from the sacrificial bowl. The consequences will be too much for me...'

Jones listened in silence, powerless.

'You may not understand it,' she continued, 'but every Bini man knows what it is to take an oath before the Uben River and later default. You'd not be buried when you die.' She suddenly became silent and turned away from Jones. 'Only God can get me out of this,' she finally muttered and gave a long sigh.

There was silence again except for the sound of their breath.

Then Jones stood up dejectedly from the bed and paced the room. It was difficult for him to accept his impotence in this matter, more because he feared loneliness than for any other reason. But what was he to do now? He had avoided all other people's company but Dolly's. He knew he was going to be paid back hard. Once or twice he had approached his tent, hearing voices chattering and laughing, but as soon as he entered, the guys quickly introduced silence or crudely changed the topic. He was mocked and caricatured behind his back; he needn't be told. And now if Dolly left, how was he to approach life here in camp? Why did he get involved in the first place? He wished he had endured. What had he entered into? There certainly was the devil's hand in this atmosphere of despair and endless idleness in camp.

Jones went to the window and pulled the white curtain aside.

There was a clear blue sky outside and the sea was the bluest he had ever seen, even in travel magazines. The skyline was calm and with many boats and ferries floating on the interminable expanse of blue. Across the thin-stretched horizon a beautiful sun nestled on vermillion and orange-coloured puffballs of cloud that rose like steam from the mountain tops. From in between the tall buildings down the beachside, Ceuta port brimmed with the bright colours of boats and ferries at the dock. This indeed was a celestial sight, a *buena vista*. But it made no impression on Jones as he let the curtains fall back in place and turned toward Dolly.

'By Friday, I believe,' he said, 'I'll have found the solution. I promise you.'

Dolly looked at him staunchly. There were tears in her eyes.

She knew they had only hours left together. Yet she couldn't tell him the whole truth; she never could. She drew the wastepaper bin to her and spat into it.

'It'll be all right,' Jones reassured her.

Dolly spat again before they left the pension[2].

---

2 Pension: a cheap hotel room for more than one person.

At ten o'clock that same evening Dolly told Jones that she was going to receive a telephone call from the madam in Italy. But she was well dressed, and she went with two other girls and Efosa. By the bridge, before the entrance to the camp, Efosa waved down a taxi, which drove them straight to a hotel in the city centre. It was a grand and shiny place and Dolly had never been to a place like that before. Soon a lady let them into Room 203. The lady was gorgeously dressed in a blue frill-studded gown and wore plenty of jewellery that clinked and glittered. She was tall and thin with a heavily made-up face and a blond weave-on that contrasted sharply with her bleached skin. She was about thirty-five although she looked much older than that.

'Come,' she said in Bini, her eyes looking searchingly at Dolly and at the other girls.

Before they could greet her she asked, 'Who is Dolly?'

'It's me,' Dolly said.

The lady looked her all over. 'I know,' she said. 'Small-sized people are a hell of a problem. I guess you are now ready to travel?' It was that same voice she had always heard over the telephone, a voice that sounded like the swish of a dagger.

'Yes, madam.' She felt an urgent need to spit but held herself.

'Good,' the lady said and drew out a pocket-sized pistol from her bra. She rubbed the cold muzzle of the pistol across Dolly's nose and said, 'You made me come down here, and that's an added expense… Hmmm – someone should have told you I'm not a free-for-all fuck. But not to worry; we'll balance the account later. Now, Efosa, get them something to eat. Emeka, take them downstairs to the cafeteria. Meanwhile, we'll be leaving tonight. Understand?'

The girls, too frightened to speak, nodded and left with Efosa.

That night at the port, the girls slipped through Immigration without the least detection. Dolly hadn't believed it would be that easy. She felt like laughing and crying at the same time. But she knew she had to wait until they had entered the port of Algeciras. And that would be in less than an hour. In less than an hour this painful throbbing of her heart would cease and the living of a dream would begin.

But shuffling through the steel-and-glass pier amidst a crowd of disorderly passengers, Dolly suddenly remembered the pocket-sized pistol and the acid glare in her madam's eyes and she shuddered. Her heart began to throb faster and faster again, faster than any dream could catch up with.

In the glass vestibule the fetid smell of the sea hit her nose.

The sudden expanse between the magnificent pier and the ferry frightened her. She observed for the first time that around the port and far into the sea were myriad lights, bright and dim, glaring and flickering. And from below the lengthy pier could be heard the uneasy shifting and rumbling of the sea. Whatever she looked at made her look so small, so insignificant. She felt dizzy. And amidst the discordant clatter of feet and luggage she felt inside her stomach a subtle sensation like the sailing of a bubble. This, too, frightened her. She dreaded to think of it or of her period, which she had missed for two weeks.

Once inside the ferry she spat again and fought her anxiety until the monstrous engine chugged off into the dark and enormous sea, toward the shadows of the Rock of Gibraltar, toward Algeciras.

The monster comes to Ceuta

Ousmane was visibly frightened. You could hear that in his breath too, as he searched the darkness around him to reassure himself that he hadn't broken altogether with reality. Then he wiped his forehead with the back of his hand and was surprised that he wasn't sweating. How did he get over that three-metre-high wall? And those cracking volleys of gunshots had not even scratched him. Allah indeed worked in mysterious ways!

Ousmane sighed and raised his head from the rag-stuffed plastic bag that was his pillow. May Allah be praised, he muttered; it was only a nightmare. He sighed and adjusted himself on the bed. Flat on his back, he stared languidly at the ceiling, still submerged in a dreamy flood of tiredness he had not felt in years. When was he ever going to get over all this; when? He had thought that the violence he had been through in the seven-month trek to this Spanish enclave of Ceuta was just some of the unwanted luggage he had thrown away at the Moroccan–Spanish border the day he had slipped in through the barbed wires. But no, this piece of luggage had followed him even into his dreams.

Sweat began to gather on his forehead. With his fingers, he felt the scrawny scar on the side of his neck and the fleshy lump by his eyebrow and winced. They were scars left by gun-toting border guards and dagger-wielding mountain robbers. On his back and buttocks were many more scars like those on his face. And they still caused him pain whenever he applied a little pressure on them, because the wounds were not well treated at the time. So Ousmane knew that even though they quickly healed on the outside, they were yet to heal on the inside. But why think of them now? He had to wait until he had crossed into the peninsula, where the best doctors would open them up again and make them heal. But for how long would he have to wait? He did not know. He had no control over his liberty and time. He just had to wait. This was all there was to it, to wait. Ousmane turned on his side for comfort and the bed creaked, loud and harsh. Of course he knew enough not to push his luck further. His bed was only a collection of plastic crates with cartons and cardboard scraps spread over them because he had neither money nor fortune enough to secure a mattress or a blanket. But he was lucky to secure a sleeping place inside one of the few tents in the camp. Some of his fellow refugees slept outside in the midnight wind and in the biting cold. He often was fortunate where or when it mattered. May Allah's name endure forever.

He rolled over carefully again and stared into the darkness. Silence floated ghost-like in the tent. Then, suddenly, the shrills of a legion of rats jolted him. He could hear them scuffle defiantly across the floor, knocking over cans and bottles and shrieking at the tops of their voices. Ousmane knew there were dozens of them in every nook and cranny of the tent, too many to be bothered about. Where had they been since he woke up? Well, he needn't bother. He must ignore them as he was already learning to do. There was no alternative. If one bothered about these rats then one wouldn't sleep at all, even in the day. Ousmane quickly turned to his mind and a subdued silence settled in the tent once more.

But Ousmane did not know what to think. The choice of thought was difficult indeed. He yawned and rattled his fingers. Lazily, he felt his groin with his hand through his trousers and further beneath his testicles. It felt so warm that his penis sprang to life immediately. But then he quickly withdrew his hand, frightened at the thought of having to think of sex all day long. Nothing was more tortuous than to arouse some desire he knew he wasn't going to satisfy. Sometimes Ousmane wished that Allah had put a switch somewhere on the human body from where he could easily switch off a surge of carnal desire that often overwhelmed him. He began to think of Guinea Conakry. Of its beautiful women. And of its many bars and nightclubs. He thought of how the nightclubs teemed with beer, cigarettes, hot drinks and roasted meat. And how the boys and the girls, the men and the women, danced heartily in the warm nights through the motley flashes of disco lights and loud music. He thought of Fatoumata, the slim one, whom he had started to date before he left. Oh, how sweet and troubling memories were! Ousmane had kissed Fatou thrice and had fondled her small mango breasts under the big mango tree by her grandma's hut in Ratoma. And these three times were the most pleasant moments of his life that he could remember. The thought of Fatoumata suddenly brought tears to his heart. She was of a different tribe, a very pretty Fula girl with small rows of ivory-white teeth. She had a smile that made you think of a gurgling spring. Fatou was like that. And always the perfume of cherry flowers in front of her grandma's hut followed her even when she had just left the foul smoke of the fireside. Ousmane couldn't figure out how she always managed to smell so lovely, but he liked it. She had a small, silky voice and an affectionate way of calling him 'Oosmane, Oosmane'. She was like a gem you did not search for but which once found, the fear of losing it kept you scared the rest of your life. Why were some girls like that, Ousmane thought. And to think that he had undertaken this journey without telling her made his situation more unbearable. It was yet the greatest pain of his life.

But I tried, he would moan whenever he remembered it, I tried. Which was true, only that on each occasion he turned back because he knew he could not face her. Instead, he began to avoid her as the day of his departure approached. Yet it was not his fault that he left. Surely it was not his fault? After the president ordered in bulldozers, soldiers and armoured tanks to destroy their house and his master's workshop in Bambino district, Ousmane and his family moved to Ratoma into his uncle's three-room house. Since then it had been hard times and harder times until his friend, Ahmadou, of the twisted teeth suggested this journey that took him away from his country and home and made him a refugee. But it seemed the world was made like that. His own fate was even better than Ahmadou's, who was caught again by the border guards and was now awaiting torture and deportation in some detention cell in Usda. It was better to be a refugee here, he reasoned. After all, every African was a potential refugee. Because African leaders, in their greed and obsolete stupidity could at any point trigger a chain of ridiculous events that would inevitably make their people refugees. In Africa, governments and leaders were like that. Well, not waiting to peruse the problem of African leadership further, Ousmane felt he knew what to do. As soon as he got to Spain and got a job, he would write to tell Fatoumata to wait for him, if only her family hadn't gotten her married to someone else. What a tradition, too!

Suddenly there was a flick and the electric bulb on the roof of the tent glared. Ousmane turned away from the menacing light and looked at his watch. It was seven thirty a.m.

'Ahh-hh, who turned on the light?' someone growled inside the tent, half-asleep.

There was a spontaneous shuffling of feet and creaking of beds as other tent mates turned away from the light as well.

'Man, put off that light! Put it off!'

'I am looking for my slippers, men. Who took my slippers?' Yemi, the noisy one, countered. 'I say, who took my slippers, eh? Who took them? Now I can see one leg, but where is the other, eh? Can somebody talk to me?'

'Man, take another slippers from anybody's bed and fuck off," growled Tony.

'Men, why are you guys fucking off me life, eh?' Yemi complained.

'Fuck off that light,' Tony snarled and, to everybody's surprise, flew up from his bed and ripped the bulb away from its socket. Yemi let out a full-throated laugh, stomped his feet intricately on the floor and, in the darkness, walked outside screaming 'fucked' and 'damned' and 'godforsaken'. Yemi was like that. Ousmane and the others had always suspected that something was mentally wrong with him, only it wasn't full-blown yet. After a thirteen-month trek through the desert and the northern mountains to this camp, he urgently needed psychotherapy. Even now Ousmane could hear him talking to himself outside.

'I need this head examined, men. You get what I mean? I am fucking sick of this animal life.'

Once again the tent became quiet. You could hear a thousand and one snores and ignore them. But the rats' noises? Impossible, certainly impossible to ignore. The manner in which they asserted their existence suddenly became an assault on your very existence. For their size, they were very loud and disquieting, with the little miscreants brushing their bodies across the crates and planks under your bed. Sometimes they jumped into the cartons where you kept your plates and spoons and rattled them annoyingly. At other times they were so impudent you had to throw a slipper angrily in their direction. The rats were like that, even in the day. You had to be menacingly close to them before they abandoned the right of way for you. Perhaps having grown bigger than normal made them trundle about with a false sense of worth. How awful they smelled, too. And with all the dust and sand and dirt they always threw out of their holes from right round the tent and from under the beds, the tent itself now had a sickening odour no one ever got used to.

Ousmane blew air through his partially blocked nose and cleared his throat. He heard Yemi shuffle back into the tent and threw himself noisily on the bed moaning, 'This fucking dog life sef!'

Ousmane's back began to ache, so he turned on his side. But somebody had taken most of the space on his bed. He felt the fellow with his hand. Whoever it was felt cold and breathed noisily. For all Ousmane knew it was not Wiwa, his tent mate, because this fellow was large and smelled of decaying vegetables. He knew that people who had no place to sleep often crept into one's bed when one had slept off. Who could it possibly be, Ousmane wondered. And this fellow was dead heavy like a coffin and could not be shifted. So Ousmane felt there was no point trying. He decided instead to reprimand him in the morning.

What time was it? Hurriedly, Ousmane got up, took his slippers in the dark and felt his way to the door. The camp lights outside were bright enough and would have been brighter but for the cold and the silence. By the side of his tent, the big dog called Calamancaro lay snoring with other smaller dogs. Ousmane rubbed his eyes and blew his nose. He would have to take the eight o'clock bus if he was to get to the police station early enough. Today he would be taking the 'criminal photos' in a long process that would lead to his receiving his documents as a legal immigrant. From the police station he would go to meet Reverend Bejar, who promised him some clothes.

This was one reverend who gave hope to the many immigrants that had met him. Even the way he looked at you at first made you feel some load was taken off your chest. Ousmane remembered having felt like that the first time he met the reverend father in his office. Of course he had felt he had no business going to see him, being a Muslim himself. But then he had gone because his friend, Paul Doe, had convinced him that the reverend was there for every asylum-seeker that needed help. It wasn't easy at first, especially when the reverend father began by asking him which denomination he worshipped with. The first instinct had been to lie, but he managed somehow to let the truth out. And thereafter the man took more than thirty minutes advising him on the problems he was sure to face as an asylum-seeker in Ceuta camp and in Spain afterwards. But when the priest told him that he must avoid contact with the use or the sale of drugs in camp he did not understand him. Not at all. He had nodded in affirmation though, hoping that Paul Doe or Sidi Diallo would explain to him later what all that meant. At least, for his troubles, Ousmane got chocolates, biscuits and a promise of a pair of trousers and shirts. That made him wonder if the imam of his mosque back home would, in a situation like this attend to an infidel, no, to a non-Muslim, the way this elderly priest had attended to him. And with a pinch of shame he concluded that it would be like a chase after the wind.

Ousmane headed down the slope where he habitually urinated. As his worn shirt flapped in the wind, he relished the sharp freshness of this morning's air. Over his head the thousands of eucalyptus trees that wooded the camp heaved and swayed.

After he had finished he went and sat on the stump of a tree in front of his tent and watched the eastern sky where the sun, not yet visible, had already painted the sailing clouds with beautiful tints of orange and amber, and in some places a thrilling purple.

Suddenly the camp began to wake up. From the surrounding tents Ousmane heard the shuffling of feet and the chattering of voices. Then there were the nauseating sounds from the blowing of noses and spitting and the crisp-voiced complaints about switching on of lights. And as the big zip locks of the tents flew open one after the other, he saw human heads pop out like rodents from shallow holes. Their heads first sniffed around the doorways like rats and then they dragged their bodies out into the cold. Immediately the similarities between the humans of Calamocarro and the rats with which they lived struck Ousmane. Besides the fact that he and his fellow refugees often busied themselves with mending and fighting over sleeping positions, the search for food was a daily affair. And like rats they easily picked short, sharp and bitter quarrels. But for the cat-like presence of the Guardia Civil in camp, blood and flame would have been a common sight. Dare to forget any of your clothes outside for an hour and they immediately disappeared as if they were in a warren of rats. And the camp was a warren in every sense. What with the thousands of trees, stones, dust and dirt tracks and peculiar odour of the waste bin and burst sewage pipes, a warren perhaps could have been better.

In all, the camp had two dormitories with toilets and a bathroom attached to each. There were about seventeen tents and numerous tin shacks. The dormitory on top of the slope was called The Whitehouse after the US seat of power. It was painted white like the one down the slope, and the older asylum seekers who lived and ran the affairs of the camp from there were considered privileged. Although stronger, safer and immune to the elements, The Whitehouse was still a burrow, but more like a burrow in the rock dug by more powerful rodents. There were numerous private tents too littering the camp alongside derelict tin shacks. But these private tents, small-sized and colourful, were actually camping tents. Ousmane was surprised that some refugees could afford the money for these tents. It would have been the best thing to do, he thought, if only he had the money himself.

There again, Allah was kind to him. Sidi Diallo, who hawked newspapers in the city, had promised to pay his bus fare to town once more, or he would have trekked the winding distance as usual. Not only that, Sidi had promised to take him to the newsagent's next week so that he could hawk newspapers himself. Not many people had opportunities like that, the opportunity to escape from tortuous hours of idleness, boredom, gossip, bickering, fighting and pennilessness. Someday, Ousmane hoped, an end would be put to all these. And Calamocarro would, like all nightmares, be dead to him, just like the four-month ordeal that had brought him to Ceuta.

Embattled by his own thoughts, Ousmane forgot about the cold and the time. He looked at his watch and began to hurry. On his way from the bathroom, he met Sidi Diallo combing his bushy hair by his tent.

'What time is it?' Sidi asked him.

'Seven forty-five.'

'Then hurry up and dress; I'll meet you in your tent now,' said Sidi.

Ousmane left. By his tent, as he spread his towel on a clothes line, he saw two men, who stood by the door of his tent and with utmost caution peered into the tent. Ousmane could see apprehension on their faces like rats whose hole had been taken over by a large snake. Just as he wondered who they were, a smallish fellow ran out of the adjacent tent liked a puzzled rat, stopped in front of Ousmane's tent, peered into it, shook his head and left. The other two men began to leave as Ousmane advanced.

'That's the monster himself,' said one of them. 'You can't mistake that bulging tummy and the capacious head.'

'Only God can save us now,' replied the other. 'There's bound to be chaos in the camp soon. Who could have harboured this animal in any tent at all?'

'I heard that his townsman lives in that tent.'

'That tent will be the doom of this camp, I tell you. How could anybody have opened his door to a boa constrictor? It beats me. Or hasn't anyone in that tent seen or heard of this guy? I can't believe it.'

'Even crocodiles have friends,' retorted his friend.

'That's where you're wrong; this is one fella that has no friends. His best friend is rotting in Assamakka jail. And it is known that he informed on him.'

'Who was the friend?'

'Felix. You don't know that black guy we once stayed with in Rabat?'

'Oh, oh, oh. I remember. Was that why I never saw that guy again?'

'Yes. He was picked up the same morning that hotel was raided. And this Ogboru was said to have been seen in a police van minutes before that raid.'

Ogboru! The name sounded like a dagger in Ousmane's ears. He held his tummy to quell the pain that erupted within. It just couldn't be true – Ogboru, here in Ceuta, in Calamocarro and in his own tent? Ousmane wished it couldn't be true. He hadn't met this Ogboru face to face. But like anyone else who, on route to Europe, had passed through Mali, Algeria and Morocco, Ousmane had heard about him. As the tale went, he was a man of monstrous potential. His credentials were indeed awesome. He was reputed to be a liar and a cheat, an informant, a con man, a forger, a swindler and a trolley. Of all that Ousmane had heard about him, it was his ability to escape revenge attacks that baffled him most. In Tangier, where Ousmane came closest to meeting him, Ogboru was said to have escaped death from hired killers by jumping to safety from his three-storey hotel room. That was exactly three days after the five Ghanaians he informed on set him up. But as a political thug in his home country and a jail-breaker in The Gambia, his escape was no mean feat. But then this failed attacked on his life resulted in a police raid that same night in Tangier and its suburbs, a raid that led to the arrest and deportation of eighty-five black immigrants, including Ousmane himself.

Ousmane's second deportation was in Agadez. Or was it even the first? He could not remember clearly now. But Ogboru was also linked to it. That night as much as Ousmane could remember, he was sleeping with four of his friends – Sidi Diallo was there too – in a filthy, windowless room the owner had rented out for the night, when suddenly there was a grating knock on the door. They woke too late to stare into the dazzling torchlights and the dark muzzles of the police guns amidst a swishing of batons. In a cramped cell later, they learnt that Ogboru was the reason for their arrest. Some of the inmates said they were aware that Ogboru had swindled an Algerian businessman out of thousands of dollars. How he did it no one knew. But that his evil schemes were always a disaster for his fellow black immigrants was well understood. Worst of all was that this Ogboru moved and lived like a ghost. Ousmane only saw those who saw him but never saw him himself. Perhaps he could have met him in Rabat, for he seemed to choose only the routes through which Ousmane travelled. But Ousmane was usually fortunate – thanks to Allah – for no sooner was it rumoured that Ogboru was seen in Sallam Motel somewhere in the suburb of Rabat than some Malians, Ghanaians and Nigerians went there and fought him until he left. And there was no doubt that their collective action saved everyone another gruelling torture session and deportation, for as was feared, many fake dollar bills were seized from him. Allah was very merciful.

And now this was the man that had suddenly surfaced in Ceuta and in his own tent. Ousmane was terribly upset. Why was he destined to be followed about by this man? How was he to avoid this pestilent creature? How, Allah, how?

But Allah did not answer.

At the threshold to his tent Ousmane hesitated. He took one foot in and his heart started to beat. Between his bed and Wiwa's, the man, Ogboru, lay snoring like a tired wild cat with his paw across his large head. Except for his swollen stomach and his remarkable skull, Ousmane could not make much out of him. And when he stirred in his sleep Ousmane took his eyes from him and looked outside. He saw two girls peering into the tent. But as Ousmane's eyes caught theirs they immediately turned away, pretending to be engaged with loftier matters.

What ill luck was this, Ousmane wondered as he prepared himself for the police station and went for Sidi Diallo.

'Is it true?' Sidi asked as soon as they met outside. 'Have you heard too that Ogboru entered this camp early this morning?'

Ousmane collected his breath. 'He is inside that tent right now.'

'Which tent?' asked Sidi.

'Our tent.'

'What? You don't mean it, do you? Who brought him there? Who?'

'I think it was Wiwa. He is lying in between our beds now.'

Sidi Diallo saw that Ousmane was visibly upset and said, "Well, until we come back, we'll see what we can do, even if you must leave that tent.'

Between them was silence as they went down the dusty road to the bus stop. Then suddenly Ousmane said, 'Sidi, I can't stand deportation again.' And there was fear in his voice.

'Not here,' said Sidi. 'He can't do any of those things here. There is the language to contend with before we're posted to the mainland, I promise you.'

Ousmane knew Sidi was merely comforting him and that didn't make his premonitions any lighter. He knew too that the camp was aflame with the news of Ogboru's arrival. At the telephone booth, at the bus stop and inside the bus, Ogboru's arrival was what everyone discussed. Perhaps, Ousmane wished, the people would rally together and drive him out as they did in Rabat. Even when Ousmane arrived at the police station, some black immigrants were already gathered together discussing the arrival of the monster. But there were hardly any solutions, as no one knew how to handle him in this new circumstance where it was forbidden to fight. For whoever fought risked being left here in camp for many months while others got posted out. Ousmane knew that Ogboru's case was a risky one like the case of the tse-tse fly that perched on a hunter's scrotum: crush it with the hate it deserved and the testicles were crushed along with it; ignore it and it would suck the hunter's veins dry. No one knew exactly what to do: to attack Ogboru or just avoid him.

As Ousmane finished his activities in the town and took a bus back to the camp, his mind still wrestled with the dangers of Ogboru's arrival. What was that guy here to do? Was he here to stay or to cook up some trolley business? Or was it for something more dangerous? Ousmane revisited his waking dream bit by bit and was convinced that Ogboru's arrival in camp was the explanation for it. May Allah thwart the progress of an infidel, he prayed. That any situation could have brought him to the point of sharing his bed with a man like Ogboru was beyond his imagination. What was Wiwa to gain from this treachery? Why was it this Ogboru that he had to bring into this tent? Wiwa always complained he had no money and needed help. But who had money? Was he expecting that this swindler could help him? Was that enough to destroy the gritty peace of the tent? Or were they actually birds of a feather? Why was the world made this way? Why was there never a peace that lasted for long? How was he, Ousmane, going to handle this problem? Would his tent mates help resist this man? Why was the world made like this?

But Ousmane got no answers. When finally the bus stopped, he trudged up the Calamocarro hill, tired and breathless, still hoping that Ogboru's arrival would turn out to be a hoax. Even when the refugees around him discussed the evil wind of Ogboru's coming, he skirted their company and lagged behind. He was that sensitive. Then on turning the bend to the entrance to his tent, Ousmane saw him!

He was sitting on the fragile car-chair in front of the tent, looking like an owl: dark-skinned, fearsome, brooding and so silently wicked. His white glasses hung on the lower ridge of his broad nose while his swindler's eyes roved around from the top of the rims. His head was large with a high forehead that seemed swollen with the machinations of unspeakable sorts.

And as it seemed too bulky to be moved at will, he kept rolling his eyes ninety degrees in their sockets like an owl. His lips were wide and black and looked comical even in their quicksand movements. All the while the wind was on the breast of his grey and rumpled coat and he held it tight so as not to expose his dirty brown shirt. And his grey trousers were dirty and rumpled too. The night trek through the mountains was quite evident on him, and he sat there in all his monstrosity, being aware of it.

Without recognising it, Ogboru's haggardness pleased Ousmane as he avoided his eyes and walked into the tent, convinced that although evil, he had come into the camp like everybody else, helpless and penniless.

Inside the tent Ousmane's tent mates sat with friends drinking from a packet of red wine and smoking cigarettes and hashish. They did not notice Ousmane. They yelled and laughed and sang Bob Marley's 'Rat Race' along with a small radio-cassette recorder. These were not the kind of people that reasoned with you, Ousmane thought and his head reeled with the smoke that swirled in the tent. How could any sane person be feasting when a poisonous snake lurked somewhere inside his room? Ousmane could not understand it at all.

Well, he knew already what to do. It was best to act by himself and leave them with their inflammable peace. He quickly began to gather his few belongings into a big plastic bag. As he tucked the lot into the head of his bed there suddenly broke out an uproar and a stampede outside, rumbling like the voice of thunder through the entire camp. Ousmane did not panic; he knew what it was. He immediately reached for his plastic plate and dashed outside. At the concrete platform behind which the refugees queued for food, a Red Cross van was parked and the food it had driven in with was being off-loaded. And from all directions the refugees hastened with plates and bowls, while those already queued up called out loudly to their friends to hurry up. Getting food was a war everybody had to cope with in camp every day, because a little delay and those Malian sharers would cart away every morsel and one would starve. This was the first lesson Ousmane had learnt in camp.

All through the afternoon, as he waited for night to come, he lay on his bed with a piece of paper fanning himself and battling with hordes of houseflies that darted about the tent. And when at last night came Sidi Diallo came too and carried the plastic bag that contained all of Ousmane's belongings. And as they had earlier agreed, they quietly dismantled Ousmane's bed of crates and cartons and took it away. And to a barrage of questions as to what was amiss, Ousmane lied that he had found a more convenient place to stay and was going to exchange that with someone else. This had been Sidi's idea, because he had reasoned that if Ousmane left like that and Ogboru occupied his position then Ogboru would have too soon a solid foothold that could imperil everybody else. It was better therefore if he remained a squatter.

So that night Sidi and Ousmane searched about the camp for any man from Mali or Zaire who had no sleeping position and who must measure no less than six feet and with muscles bulky and raw enough to intimidate the monster. Their lot finally fell on a Zairean called Mtumba. And immediately they took him to Ousmane's tent and showed him his new position and hoped he could, physically at least, handle the imminent challenges ahead.

And as Ousmane for the last time stepped across the threshold of his tent and went outside, he still felt that his worries were far from over. He was convinced that the worst for sure was yet to come now that this monster had at last come to Ceuta.

Murder in Camp

Calamocarro camp in Ceuta was frighteningly quiet that midnight in November. Maybe it was always like that when somebody was going to die. Chike was restless. He knew what was going to happen; the informant was going to die. Although he was not going to be directly involved with the killing, the plot had his consent. And that was as weighty on his mind as the act itself. He had not imagined that the last minutes of a plot like that could be this disquieting. He wished he could drink a can of beer to distort the detailed images of probable consequences that played themselves out on his mind. But he resented the fever that was bound to come the following morning. His system was like that – a quaff of alcohol and he'd be knocked out the next day. He lit a cigarette instead and went outside the tent.

A cold breeze enveloped him and he realised that he had been sweating. He wiped his forehead with his thumb and peered into the dark and misty surroundings. There weren't many folks outside as was often the case and, in the direction of the camp secretary's tent, the number of people watching the late-night movie had dwindled. Soon the secretary's assistant would pack up the TV set and take it inside and everywhere would be completely quiet and set for the plot to hatch. It was only a matter of an hour or two. He kicked the earth in front of him and began to pace the frontage of his tent, blowing smoke into the damp air. He was nervous; this night the informant was going to die.

Despite the breeze he still felt a sad stillness in the air that hung over the camp. It was burdensome and oppressive and he could not explain it. Behind him, by the foot of his tent, a big rat was busy throwing out sand and stones from its hole while other rats scurried here and there shrieking piercingly. And already the smell of fresh and wet earth had replaced the usual odour of the waste bin. It wasn't particularly cold tonight, Chike thought. But he knew that the weather was not to be trusted.

Even the few refugees who had not gone to bed yet knew that too, as they went about the shadows in their thick sweaters and rumpled jackets. There was hardly any sound of laughter anywhere. Nor were there the small gatherings of friends who often sat and talked together in loud and hope-filled voices. It was dull and dreary wherever he looked and the poorly lit paths gave him the feeling of treading through the land of the living dead. It was for him a scene too tortuous to bear, coupled with the fury of the betrayal he had tried to contain since the events of these past days.

Four days had gone but at least he and his friends had been able to find out who the informant was. At first everybody had thought that it was Gideon Ogboru, that notorious informant of Tangier and Algiers, the monster himself, who had entered this camp a few weeks ago. But when it turned out that the informant was a character everyone trusted, even the people who had no stakes in the business were infuriated. Who would have thought that the camp secretary could have done a thing like that? But then envy was capable of any evil. Whatever Chike and his friends considered pointed to the fact that not only could the secretary have done it but that he did.

The weekend before the Guardia Civil raided the camp, the secretary was said to have stayed with a friend, asking him who sold hashish in camp. Chike heard that he even went ahead pointing out to this friend of his those he suspected himself. And he had boasted that he was going to kill off 'this business that makes those anglophone boys swollen-headed'. He was said to have the telephone number of the police and the Guardia Civil. Not only that, everybody in camp had heard too, or had heard from somebody who had heard that the police had promised him a job in their office in Madrid if he was seen to be devoted and helpful. Because Spain was not a place an immigrant got a job like that, a promise like that could turn a man's head in any direction, Chike thought. But to have turned against his fellow suffering brothers in a refugee camp was one betrayal too many. Why hadn't he warned the people first, as he was supposed to? Too bad, Chike concluded; a white man could always turn a black man against one of his own for a plate of porridge. And this secretary was a Gambian who claimed Sierra Leonean nationality. Some folks even said he was Senegalese. But it was difficult to tell people's true identity in camp because immigrants, for fear of deportation, often claimed the nationalities of countries at war. That notwithstanding, Chike believed that he was Senegalese because of the company he kept and for his very dark skin. His name was Saidu Sembene. But in camp everybody called him El Secretario.

He was tall and lean and very sluggish in his manners except when he answered to the authorities. He had eyes as small as a pig's, which darted about and perched on yours as if they were sincere, even when he was lying through his teeth. And that soft-spoken nature of his was one big deception too. Not only had the refugees in camp fallen for it but it had also equally deceived the police and the Guardia Civil who dealt with the refugees. For instance, if there was any fracas at all in camp you would hear the camp guards shouting, 'Secretario! Secretario! Donde estas?' And if he appeared, what he said was what they believed. And this often put the English-speaking refugees at a disadvantage because he often favoured the francophone refugees with tent allocations and appointments in camp. People had been murmuring for a long time and friction had always been averted by the cat-like presence of the camp guards. And now it had come to this. Just because he manipulated the French language and picked up a little Spanish, he had taken up the job of an informant. He had gone too far this time and somebody was going to make him pay for it.

The more Chike thought about this the more he grew annoyed. He threw away the butt of his cigarette and lit another. The bastard, he spat; what business was it of his if people sold hashish? Could you imagine a common refugee like everybody else trying to lord it over everyone in camp? What exactly did he and the authorities expect everybody to do in this wretched and idle place? Fold their hands all day long in soul-breaking idleness? Or take up sticks and chase rats around the camp? Surely everybody couldn't go to town washing cars and vending newspapers, especially when there was something else that kept them busy and gave them money. Just because the secretary hadn't nerve enough did not mean that he should inform on those who had. The bastard. You couldn't think of what his actions had cost the camp without wanting him dead. He deserved anything, Chike fumed, anything that could be visited on him tonight. Every thick inch of it!

The camp indeed had lost the little colour it had. Anyone could easily see how dull and solemn the nights had become. Now people went to bed before it was midnight, unlike when music was heard loud and clear and people drank and danced away boredom and despair until about two in the morning. There were free drinks and cigarettes provided by those who did business in camp and by those peddlers who came from the peninsula and made use of the camp girls too. Now that precarious life had collapsed since the Guardia Civil had raided the camp and carted away the merchandise along with all the money they could find in everyone's bags. Indeed, everyone's happiness went with that raid. Two people were taken away and put in detention while the authorities still came every day to arrest more people. And there was such a fear in camp that no one knew who would be fingered next.

That notwithstanding, the security agents had added insult to injury by an inaccurate reporting of what had happened. After they had searched everywhere and taken all the money, they told the press that they had found only six hundred and sixty-six thousand pesetas. To Chike that was a pathological lie because he knew that he himself had lost nearly six hundred thousand. Big Daddy alone lost nine hundred and fifty-six thousand. Lincoln lost six hundred and ninety thousand; Quintero lost six hundred and seventy-nine thousand; Yeboah lost six hundred and thirty-eight thousand; Jackie lost four hundred and seventy-four thousand-; Sam lost two hundred and eighty-nine thousand and tens of hundreds of others lost below a hundred thousand. You couldn't just accept a figure like that; but what could you do? And they had told the press, too, that only sixty-six kilos of hashish were seized, when in fact it was over one hundred and twenty kilos. The camp now mourned both the loss of livelihood and the painful boredom and hopelessness ahead.

The more Chike thought of this the more the gall spilled into his blood. Why did all this happen, he asked himself over and over again. All because one villager from Senegal happened to become a secretary in a refugee camp and spoke a little Spanish. Now, how was one to manage the life here? No one gave you soap or a sponge, brush or toothpaste. No toiletries, no clothes, no mattresses, no beds, no blankets. And certainly no money. No one gave you anything except food, which if you didn't manipulate the queue you got none, because the number swelled every day and those Malian sharers took triple rations. How long was this going to last? And how long the stay here in this town called Ceuta? The hopes that Padre Bejar's sermons raised every Sunday dampened as you left his church and the *centro* for the isolated and rotten grove called the camp. His admonitions that they avoid any contact with drugs provided no alternative. There were no recreations or petty jobs to fill up one's idle moments. And no one ever tried to keep those big-time Moroccan-Spanish dealers away from the refugees. It all came down to blame-the-immigrant syndrome because the authorities could not claim ignorance of who owned the merchandise. Or that the needy refugees were merely being used as petty peddlers. Ceuta, after all, had no big factories or multinational companies, yet the cosy lifestyle and the exotic and flashy cars and houses abounded. Nobody would probe a thing like that, nobody. Instead, the raid on a refugee camp made the front-page news. Simply because one Senegalese villager came to camp and turned informant. Plague on him.

All the more infuriated, Chike threw the butt of his cigarette away. He took out his handset and dialled Lincoln's number. Someone picked up the phone at the other end.

'Lincoln?' he asked.

'Yes?'
'So what's the situation?'
'All right; I'm in position,' said Lincoln.
'Where's Chukky?'
'They've gone to cut the wires.'
'All right; get Osili and Freddy into position, too.'
'Okay.'

Chike switched off his handset and walked towards the block dormitory called The Whitehouse. His mind grew heavier by the minute. What was he going to do in that windowless dormitory? Who was he going to see? He diverted into the lavatory, but the pungent smell of urine and excreta drove him out. He turned again towards his tent but walked past it. The consequences, the consequences, his head ticked.

The consequences would certainly be grave. First, there would be mass arrests, and everybody could be left in this camp to rot, while the documents that brought him here could be suspended indefinitely, and God knew what else could happen. And just yesterday the police and the Red Cross gave notice of an intended posting for the weekend. This plot would certainly put a stop to everything, whether it failed or succeeded. Wouldn't a riot be better after all? God, there was something in the shedding of blood that made things worse. Not that he cared about this Saidu Sembene's life. Nor that the sight of blood in itself was repugnant to him. No. His greatest fear instead lay in the possibility of being left in this soul- crippling camp for months. Nothing frightened him as much. That alone was why he had argued extensively about the timing when this plot was in the hatching. But the majority had overruled him and he didn't want to appear cowardly. The informant had to be taught the lesson that there was something of a mafia in all drug dealings, whether they were done in a refugee camp or not. And this lesson had to be taught immediately so that others would learn the wisdom of an ass.

Walking to and fro in the shadows between the rows of tents, Chike noticed a sudden sparking of lights behind the francophone section and knew that someone was attempting to cut the circuit. A flood of blood gushed through his veins and his heart began to throb. He wished in his heart, in spite of himself, for something to abort this plot – anything at all! God, what was happening to him? He wished he could just walk up to Lincoln and tell him to suspend further action for the night. But could he convince Chukky? Or Jackie? Or Yeboah? And hardest of all would be Big Daddy, who would take it personally and feel betrayed. Why was life so treacherous that one could not always take personal action on things that concerned him? Fate alone always seemed to hold all the aces, Chike decided, and he waited to see its next move.

As for him and his friends, the plot was simple. Disconnect the lights and throw away the wires. Wait for five minutes to ensure they weren't reconnected. Then four people would storm the secretary's tent, pour melted balm on his face, daze him with blows to the head, drag him out to the edge of the hillside, stab him and throw him down. If he survived the fall, he wouldn't be able to identify his attackers. And of course, his tent mate would be too panic-stricken and sleepy-eyed to come to his defence. It was that simple, and nothing, they hoped, could go wrong.

Chike's thoughts still jostled within him when the lights went out and threw the camp into darkness. He quickly tiptoed to the camp gate to monitor the movements of the camp guards. As soon as he took a position beside a tin shack bathroom at the edge of the hillside, he observed that the streetlamp nearby was growing dull, because a blanket of fog was slowly uncurling from on top of the trees across the camp. And the Guardia Civil Jeep by the camp gate was already enshrouded in this advancing fogginess. Chike felt helpless, because even the elements seemed to collude. He looked at his watch but, in the darkness, he saw nothing.

And time ticked away slowly but steadily, while the silence that accompanied it allowed only for the piercing shrills of the insects that rang deep in the pits of his ears.

Then suddenly a stillness descended from nowhere and sailed like cold through his bones. Chike's eyes darted left and right, up and down. Nothing moved but shadows, gloomy and ghostly shadows that heaved back and forth, expanded and contracted. And in the fog-muffled lights of the lampposts, the camp stewed in mist like a derelict churchyard. Chike thought he heard a scuffle and a catcall. He listened hard. But it was silence that he heard, walking about in quaking boots. He reached for his handset. But then he heard the clanging of metal and the ruffling of polythene bags. From the valley on the left, the deep, husky barking of a dog rose and echoed, and the stray dogs in the camp picked it up and began to bark. A couple of footfalls pounded the earth in the direction of the secretary's tent. Chike's heart quickened. There was no need to telephone Lincoln now, and he put the handset back in his pocket. And as the sound of the scuffle became louder, he left his position to verify it, fearing that the camp guards might hear it and proceed to intervene. On getting to the row of tents in which the camp secretary lived, he saw ahead of him two men holding another by the scruff of the neck and dragging him about while another man pummelled him with punches from behind.

It was dangerous to fail now, Chike thought and rushed to help. As he closed in, the guy who was being beaten broke away and ran towards him. And wasting no time, Chike released a bare-knuckle explosion across his forehead. The guy stumbled on impact, swung sideways and fell on a heap of wet faggots. Whimpering and twisting with pain he shouted in Arabic, 'Abdulkadir, Abdulkadir! Call the guardia; they are killing me!' The guy was clearly an Arab and not the camp secretary. Chike was bewildered. He looked at the guys, who had again circled their victim around the faggots. And he could not recognise any of them.

'What has the guy done?' he asked in truncated French, disappointed.

'Stealing towels,' one of them quickly said, breathing loudly. 'Look at that heap over there. We had been monitoring him.'

And immediately they began to beat him again, and his voice was heard even louder across the camp as he cried, 'Abdulkadir, call the guardia!' Chike saw that people had started coming out of the surrounding tents and left. He walked straight to his own tent and into his bed. But he could not sleep.

In the growing noise outside he heard the Guardia Civil shouting above every other noise, 'Secretario! Secretario! Donde estas?' Secretary, Secretary! Where are you? Chike knew those Spanish words too well and sulked. The camp secretary was still very much relevant, so he felt a lingering bitterness in his mouth. He knew then that the power in camp could not be shifted tonight and perhaps never could. He turned to the other side of his noisy bed and sighed. He was neither happy nor sad, yet a rotten feeling sat heavy in his chest.

It was some time in the middle of April. And Conakry was burning. About forty degrees or thereabouts, even though I was not used to measuring a hot day in Celsius. It was mild, hot, too hot or intolerably hot. In Guinea Conakry it was intolerably hot! It didn't help matters either that one tried to avoid the sun by walking under the shadows of the ubiquitous mango trees that lined the streets and lanes of Conakry. When it was this hot in Guinea the heat seeped through all spaces, nooks and crannies and even through ant holes. So I knew what awaited us – Kayode and I – when our taxi signalled right and sped up the highland towards Petit Simbayat district. The hot wind from the side windows burned like air from a smith's bellows, unsettling us with terse, fricative sounds like the steady crunch of dry leaves. As we neared our house my colleague, Kayode, began to point out large-bottomed girls swinging their hips by the sides of the road, while I racked my brain thinking out precise French words that would convey to the driver where to stop us. Being the one who understood and spoke a little French, much was certainly going to depend on me throughout this journey.

'Arrêt ici,' I suddenly blurted out. It was more of a command than the well-mannered request I had intended to make. Good enough that the taxi driver wasn't interested in the manners of his passengers, as he quickly jabbed on the brakes and skidded to the side of the road, stopping abruptly beside a wide-open gutter. Instantly a burst of orange dust rose from behind and filled the car, smoking us out into the sun.

Blinded by the sun and the swirling dust I managed to hand over to the driver the four thousand Guinean francs I was holding. He handed me back one thousand Guinean francs' change immediately, as if he were expecting it, and drove off in a thick cloud of orange dust.

We jumped out of the dust, over the open gutter, across the heaps and litter of rocks on every side and picked our way through the dusty and rocky track to our house, while the sun sat like a burden on our heads and shoulders. We walked blindly, beating the dust out of our bodies and clothes, while behind us, on the new asphalt under construction, cars and Jeeps swished through the hot wind as they tested out their turbo strength for all to see. Towards the sea from where we came, the old road under reconstruction gleamed new and black and, like a thread, tapered far down, across a construction site premises twirling in the dusty sun. This construction site had its wire-fenced compound littered with twenty- and forty-foot containers as far as the eye could see. And from where the road wound its way to Nongo, to Kipe, to Ratoma and to Kaporo toward en ville, the wood was thick and green and mainly of mango trees. And here and there new houses sprang up in the sun before our eyes, defiant of the dust and the heat. Somewhere on the left lived Ka'ade – Madam Fatoumata's niece – along with her two boisterous kids, Mouktar and Montaga. And sitting heavy on top of the woods, just below the cloud, was the Atlantic Ocean, misted and dark along the horizon. Seen here from the Petit Simbayat heights, this ocean was an enthralling sight. And suddenly, in spite of the sun, the heat and the dust, a soothing breeze began to sweep across this rocky and dusty plain.

Then impulsively, simultaneously, Kayode and I fumbled out our packets of cigarettes, lit one each and sucked greedily on them. There were hens by the side of the track to our house, chuckling and pecking through the sand as we approached. Suddenly a smallish bright-crested cockerel came and established itself amongst them. And from nowhere a much bigger cockerel flew down from behind us like a small tornado and chased it across the asphalt and flew back, showing itself off. What a show it made of its gallantry before the hens. And what attention it received from them before they turned once more to their chuckling and pecking. Sporadic calls of birds could be heard every now and then. The wind ceased to blow. And although pockets of breeze still came and went, the scent of dust and hot earth got stronger as we advanced towards the shadows of mango trees ahead. I relished without haste the taste of my St. Moritz, while Kayode dragged on his Benson & Hedges to its butt and lit another. What a relief was the flavour of vice! I had dreamt everyday of quitting smoking. But, God, when would that day come? Perhaps when I finally got to Europe; perhaps when all these pressures of travel had gone. And what a relief we had had today for the first time in two weeks! What a relief indeed to have been able to take the passport photographs for the international passports at the immigration office that day. What a relief indeed!

It wouldn't be curious for anyone reading through this to want to know what we were doing here in Guinea Conakry, five nations away from my own country. The answer is simple: the quest to travel to Europe had brought us this far in search of visas. As a pariah state under the murderous dictatorship of General Sani Abacha, even well before him, Nigeria became a degenerate nation, whose citizens were denied visas and legal travel documents at the mere sight of the colour of their passports. Now therefore our desire for a better economic future outside our country had to be matched by a tough-hearted adventure and a die-hard will to achieve it through extra-legal means. (And whose were those legal means anywhere?) It was an adventure risk-laden on all sides, but there was hardly any other option. Travel to a distant country, obtain travel documents and get a genuine visa put on them. Sounds ingenious. And perhaps a little easier? But that's when the tricky part of the travel actually begins for the migrant. And for the first phase, and to our greatest relief we had succeeded in applying for our international passports that day, after weeks of futile rigmarole and a waste of a lot of money in search of reliable contacts and agents to help us pull it off. So what a relief indeed today's affair had been!

Much more of a relief it was, too, when the sun suddenly eased from our shoulders as we entered the shadows of young mango trees lining the left side of the road. Still sucking on our cigarettes, we talked about Conakry main town, its buildings and its people, its attractive women and their provocative mode of dressing. We discussed Ichinini, our guide, who was our host's nephew. Ichinini was rather an eccentric guy in many ways. We laughed over his poor English, his funny gestures and his aborted attempts yesterday to secure us some girls at the discotheque. He was fun-loving but too shy to perform the role of a pimp. Just like Kayode, my colleague, he was too easily distracted to concentrate on any serious issue for long, so I wasn't disappointed that we didn't go home with any girl at all. I supposed this was why he got on much better with Kayode, even though he didn't smoke at all. And his unbridled desire to bring up a story or two about girls in every discussion was a binding factor between them.

As the blue iron gate of the compound where we lived came into sight, I remembered that before we left for town in the early hours of the morning, our hostess, Fatoumata, had told us that some men had been moved into the main building in our compound at midnight. She had called them the president's guests because President Lansana Conte had received them as asylum-seekers after having been forced out of government by the ECOMOG forces supporting President Tejan Kabba in Sierra Leone. She said the deal was to keep them away from the battlefield while the ECOMOG forces fought to restore to power the government they had ousted. Their safety was guaranteed if they didn't interfere in the peace talks already in place. And they had kept away so far. So this new accommodation had finally been allocated to them, hoping that peace would soon be found after a series of talks with them. And so with them this hope had been kept alive, the hope to bring to an end this bloody ethnic war which was killing and mutilating millions of Sierra Leonians.

Now coming back from town and headed for the gate was when we saw them beside a small windowless round hut, beneath a small mango tree, in front of a small bush that rolled down a small valley behind them, from where all the wind seemed to blow. But there were only two of them at first – Dr Johnson, the rebel ex-mayor of Freetown, who sat on a small three-legged stool, bald-headed, bare-bodied and in regular white shorts, a striped brown shirt hanging on his shoulder with which he intermittently chased away meddlesome flies. The other was a colonel, the secretary to Paul Koromah's ECOMOG-ousted military junta, called Colonel Sese.

Both men were especially jovial and friendly and it made you wonder how they managed not to carry their colossal misfortune on their faces like the one they called the ex-chief judge who always wore a gloomy face swollen with the misfortune of having to relinquish power and learn to be a tolerable fugitive. They called him the Old Antelope too, probably because of his wisdom and constant brooding. His colleagues said too that he had serious diabetic issues, and you would wonder what use his wisdom was as he gulped down chilled Coca-Cola soft drinks every day. The other rebel soldier we were yet to meet was a jolly fellow called Colonel Nelson. He was medium-sized, nearly as fat as the ex-chief judge and nearly always smiling. You couldn't imagine him a soldier at all if no one told you he was one. In his quest to learn French fast, Colonel Nelson had captured in a few words what I supposed was the philosophy of his present dilemma and used it as a form of greeting amongst his fellow rebel commanders whom he would greet, Comme ci, comme ça,' and they would reply, 'C'est la vie.' Colonel Nelson was a man who smiled more than he talked, unlike Dr Johnson and Colonel Sese, who were quite communicative. But he was a sharp contrast to the ex-chief judge, who hardly talked at all, and when he did, it was only with his pretty, big-bottomed girlfriend, who nearly always stayed with him. They were such a cheerful bunch though that in just a few days I became acquainted with them all, except with the Old Antelope, who fenced himself off thoroughly with his taciturnity and unrelenting brooding.

A week later when Kayode and I were coming back from town we met Dr Johnson and Colonel Sese on that same spot by the road toward our compound. They seemed happy to see us, apparently already bored conversing amongst themselves all day long. As their faces lit up, I knew that we were a welcome distraction.

'Bonjour, Doctor et Colonel,' I greeted them both. The Colonel held a small transistor radio to which they listened half-hourly. It was always on the BBC's *Focus on Africa*.

'Cava?' said the Doctor.

'Cava, bien merci, et vous?' I chorused with Kayode.

'Très bien, mes amis, très bien,' said the Colonel, smiling and putting the radio on the ground in between some tufts of grass.

'How is en ville? Had a nice time?' asked Dr Johnson with a perpetual smile on his face and sprinkles of white hair on his head and moustache. 'The town? I mean the town; how did you find it?' His smile was infectious.

'Il fait chaud, très chaud aujourd'hui. The sun was unrelenting! If not for occasional spells of breeze... A small but an orderly town. Nice in its own way – not much traffic, sane drivers, too...'

'Certainly not like your Lagos,' put in the young colonel, all smiles.

'Yeah yeah,' I owned up, 'not at any length near Lagos.'

'Lagos, is it?' persisted the colonel, his eyes darting limpidly like a reflection of light on spring water. His cheeks were all smiles and his small teeth shone with the intense whiteness of a coconut. He sat up from the hammock and we shook hands as if we were paying our respects to the chaotic life in Lagos and accepting its supremacy in this respect. Soon Kayode left us, having sensed that we would be delving into political topics that bored him. We talked about the heat and the dust of Conakry and about many things more. Dr Johnson talked about their new life in this Petit Simbayat neighbourhood, to which they fought to adapt. One could hear his voice, clear and elitist, in the intermittent gusts of breeze that swept by us.

'Ibo,' the young colonel suddenly cajoled me after the name of my tribe in Nigeria, 'your man has done it again!'

'Who?'

'Your president, Abacha. He has just disrupted a pro-democracy rally in Ibadan. They said he infiltrated it from within and broke it up with his own supporters. How does he manage that, getting thousands of people to carry anti-democracy placards? Yet you Nigerians complain you don't want him.'

'We call it rent-a-crowd,' I said. 'To whoever attended he paid enough for a day's meal. Babangida taught him that: rent a crowd, call the press and hand out brown envelopes and it becomes world news. And soon all the big vultures land to spread it about – the BBC, CNN; name them.'

'Kai,' he shook his head. 'African rulers – there is no stopping them.'

'You mean what you just said?' asked Doctor Johnson naively. 'That he actually goes out to buy these people to chant his praises?'

'For all I know, Doc, the art of praise-singing only witnessed a slight modification and... it's not un-African,' I argued. 'The BBC said he spent six million dollars on that youths' rally he staged at Abuja two weeks ago.'

'Six million dollars!' This time the ex-mayor was clearly alarmed.

'The megalomaniac has a lot of oil money to play with, you know. Six million is a mere pittance to him; millions and millions of dollars disappear every day. Ask questions and you disappear alongside these bags of money. Or assassins simply come and blow you up, even if you are cornered in a market place.'

'Really?' This time it was from the young colonel. 'But that's not the image we get of your country, even when I went through Jaji Military School in Nigeria. You watch CNN and you see a different thing. Road constructions. Good living conditions from Lagos to Abuja and everywhere. Placard-carrying Nigerians chanting pro-government slogans. But of course we hear of fuel scarcity, convulsive power supply, armed robberies and professional assassinations; besides which, every other thing goes on fine.'

And so we chatted on while the ex-mayor kept shaking his head with its accompanying greyness. Kayode joined us again, still sucking on a cigarette. The colonel had a distant look in his eyes, while I kept shifting my weight from one leg to the other as I tried to soothe the heat that discomforted us. And over Conakry the sun hung heavily, leaving no one in doubt as to who was in control here.

'Going on fine indeed,' I said. 'Perhaps you are only a military man, but you should know it is all propaganda. I'm neither for the politicians nor for a military dictatorship. It's all a vicious cycle to me – military–civilian, civilian–military. But this Abacha is the worst of all the beasts we have had in decades. So crude, so brutish, so barbaric. And he is the least tactful. When he goes out to kill his opponents he doesn't care if they are in a marketplace; he just hacks them down right there in front of everybody. You saw how he murdered Ken Saro-Wiwa and the others while the Commonwealth meeting was in session in Auckland? Even Idi Amin in his days wouldn't do a thing like that. And we know obviously what lies behind all those money-guzzling rallies and assassinations.'

'And what could that be? To succeed himself?' asked the ex-mayor.

'For sure. And he will succeed himself unless, if by a miracle, he dies. He has laid all machinery ready to swear himself in as a civilian president.'

'What makes you think that?'

'Everything he's ever done: all the arrests and detentions, the intimidations and all those government-funded rallies, etcetera, were all geared towards that.'

The ex-mayor of Freetown, Dr Johnson, looked at the colonel, winced and shook his head.

'There is no reprieve in sight,' he said. And turning toward me, he continued, 'That man is ruthless. Imagine a president talking about another president like this: When we have finished with John Koroma... we will catch him and we will "deal" with him. Not once did he say that, not twice, but several times.'

As he winced again and stopped talking abruptly, the resigned and confused stares in their eyes told me immediately that their fate and that of their rebel colleagues still holding out in the diamond-rich Kono district of Sierra Leone were somewhat tied to the leadership chaos back home in my country, where our brutal dictator was taking all devilish and anti-democratic options possible to thwart a return to democratic rule. It was evident that these rebels, more than Nigerians even, wished Sani Abacha dead or removed from office.

The sun still burned with no less intensity over Conakry. And the dust rose now and then in sudden puffs, whipped up by tiny pockets of whirlwinds. All one saw were rocks, heaps of stones and dust-covered leaves and a few lazy dogs on the prowl. A gust of breeze rattled the mango leaves above us so vigorously that we thought a monkey was at play. The smallish old woman who owned the hammock on which the young colonel sat came out of her small hut with a walking stick and smiling toothlessly greeted us, 'Jarama nane.'

'Bonsoir,' we replied in unison, even though we were sure that she spoke only her native Fula. And as soon as she went back into her round windowless hut, the colonel looked at his wristwatch and picked up the transistor radio from beneath the hammock.

'Is it the hour?' Dr Johnson asked.

'More or less,' he replied and turned the ON knob.

And immediately William Marshall's voice went up in the air, on the BBC's *Newsdesk*. There was the bit on Tony Blair's Middle East visit. And there was the news on the Rwanda–Burundi genocide trials going on in Arusha, Amnesty International's condemnation of the gross violation of human rights in Nigeria and the recent assassination of a senior military officer also in Onitsha, Nigeria.

'There is nothing on us,' Dr Johnson said resignedly with a squint in one eye. The young colonel nodded and the ex-mayor stood up abruptly. 'Well, gentlemen,' he announced, 'I'll go back to study; time lost is never regained. I'll try to make myself more useful. See you all later.'

He left. Kayode and I prepared to leave too, while the colonel, grappling with his studies in languages, lay back in the hammock, taking John Smith's *Je Me Debrouille En Anglais* along with him.

Again we welcomed a new day in Guinea Conakry. To say the least, mornings were generally cool here with the sea breeze sweeping over the city like balm and leaving one with an exaggerated feeling of ennui. Oftentimes one fondled the feeling that a tempestuous rainfall was imminent. But today the sky did not give out any remarkable impression at all; it was just one interminable dome of motionlessness, of mist and ash-coloured clouds. The electric lights were burning bright, brighter by far than the half-lights we have in Nigeria. A strong scent of Raid insecticide hung heavy in our room, an acrid reminder of the chemical attack on mosquitoes of the night before. And every now and then the clucking of wild pigeons sailed musically through the morning mist alongside the piercing crows of the gallant cocks of the neighbourhood. Then, surprise-surprise, as you stepped out across the door you found out that the Conakry houseflies had woken up before you, darting about in nauseating droves even before the hordes of mosquitoes of the previous night had begun a desperate and clumsy flight to escape a scorching sun that was sure to rise.

If Fatou, our hostess, kept her promise of bringing us some mosquito nets today from Aissatou, her niece, then I would escape forever this blood-sucking scourge of Africa's urban cities. My nights had become tortuous with several waking-ups at midnights to kill off some of these mosquitoes while Kayode snored like a drunk. I had thought that our change of cigarettes to the readily available ones was responsible for the general bodily weakness Kayode had been complaining about. But the sight of these mosquitoes with blood-swollen tummies made me think that we might become victims of malaria fever any time soon. Not only had these mosquitoes bitten their way into our veins, they had bitten their way into my dreams too. Cruel, tiny vampires!

I had woken up feeling a little feverish and had believed that a cold shower could resolve it. But the sight of these mosquitoes began to resurrect the nightmares I had been through lately. They had been persistent, recurrent and frightening. I had had similar nightmares lately; so similar had they become that wishing them away as mere symptoms of malaria fever would not make sense any more. It suddenly dawned on me that these nightmares were taking on a peculiar pattern in which I was always caught up in an ambush in some countryside with some rebel soldiers shooting, maiming, killing and beheading civilians. How I always managed to escape this carnage was one of those mysteries that only dreams could explain. However, I always woke up exhausted and gasping for breath, relieved and glad that it had only been a dream.

Not once, not twice but many times had my mind explored other possible reasons for these recurrent nightmares. Yesterday, after having been asked for a cigarette by the tall policeman who sat as guard for the ex-mayor and his colleagues, it hit my mind that the Sierra Leonian government might send an assassination squad after them. That meant that I and the other tenants could easily be targeted mistakenly. Since then, I began to live my most frightening moments in Conakry. I began to focus on the gate more often to see who came in and who went out. And whenever there were heavy footfalls that tarried outside the gate, I waited with anguish for an assault of explosives, gunshots, screams, stampedes and panic. I reckoned that this fear more than anything else must have been feeding these nightmares. And the sheer impotence of not knowing how to combat it was not helping matters either. Another obvious reason was the frequent BBC–VOA–CNN news of genocide, massacres, starvation, torture, ethnic killings, lootings, terrorist bombings and armed insurrections from Kosovo to Algeria, Sierra Leone to Nigeria through the Democratic Republic of Congo to Burundi and Rwanda, where man's brutish and murderous instincts played themselves out daily on this savage earth.

Come to think of it, I said to myself, how come these Sierra Leonian gentlemen were not as apprehensive as I was? What monstrosity! They just didn't seem to care. As if they were not a security risk. They went about where and when they pleased, received guests –men and women alike – and laughed with abandon at lewd jokes they made. As if they weren't the cause of the looting, carnage, starvation and a ferocious war raging like wildfire through the cities, towns, villages and jungles of Sierra Leone. Except for the sickly ex-chief judge, I had never seen any of them thoughtful and morose.

What seemed to matter most to them in the whole universe was the small transistor radio each carried with him as if it were a kitten. And BBC's *Newsdesk* and *Focus on Africa* were their common addiction as their moods swung between war and peace. If the ECOMOG forces were said to be inflicting heavy losses on the ruling junta, they clutched their radios solemnly and sweated. But if their colleagues back home were said to be resisting valiantly, the sun would break on their faces and glee would shine in their eyes. And presently, as I knew them more, they didn't appear the monsters I had imagined weeks ago when I heard with dismay the coup d'état that overthrew the democratic government of President Tejan Kabbah. Neither did they look like the swashbuckling soldiers and dim-witted politicians we had in Nigeria. They looked more to me now like ordinary men who merely had an unpleasant brush with misfortune. Whatever influence and power they must have wielded over the lives of their fellow countrymen prior to their exile just didn't seem to matter any more. And I hadn't mustered the courage yet to ask them the ultimate question: why did they do it? Why did they plan that coup d'état? Why didn't they negotiate themselves out of power like the Haitian junta when they saw the forces opposed to them? Why did they wait to be booted out?

Or maybe it wasn't that I lacked the courage to find out. Maybe it meant that if I hadn't shown interest or sympathy that I shouldn't be seen to be curious either. I decided to take my time, believing that they would need to talk beyond themselves when the time came. Patience would play a part in this, too. So I took my own world-receiver radio, shot a glance at Kayode, who was still asleep, and went for the door.

It was cold outside. And towards the new asphalt it was grey and dusty as well. The breeze came from the sea and combed through the leafy mango trees. The grasses were withered and brown with dust. Surprisingly there were no dogs on the prowl. And you couldn't see the sea through this mist and dust. On the asphalt, a Jeep zoomed up the road and a truck full of rocks roared after it. Theirs were the only sounds you heard, otherwise it was as quiet as a Saturday morning in the countryside. Near the signpost for a nearby refugee school a boy and a girl in red tracksuits came jogging towards the rocky road where a new American embassy was being built. On the other side of the road a woman with a toddler tied to her back walked, chanting a lullaby. She was closely followed by a girl of about fifteen carrying an empty basket on her head. She was naked from the waist up and her small, unripe breasts pointed out the way in front of her. They walked through the rocks, stones and dust strewn everywhere. They walked so calmly, so unperturbed, as if the hustle and bustle of the city a few kilometres away had nothing whatsoever to do with them, as if the sun quietly pushing through the mist could never finally unleash its heat on their backs before it was noon.

Again I dragged myself through a long and dreary day, tuned in every now and then to the BBC. I chatted with the Sierra Leonian refugees I met at the local pub. I drank Fanta tonic and smoked lots of St Moritz. I then shuffled back to the house when the sun came out strongly at nine. The compound was dead quiet and would remain so until midday because everybody slept late and woke up late. Kayode was still fast asleep. But Fatoumata certainly was not. I could hear her gentle movements in the bathroom. Then I heard a soft knock on the door and turned towards the wall and pretended to be asleep. Soon Fatoumata was in the living room chatting with her niece, Aissatou, who had come with her red Toyota Celica to take her to town. As soon as they left, I made myself a cup of tea, ate, bathed and lay in bed again flicking through old *Time*, *Newsweek* and *The Economist* magazines that Colonel Nelson had loaned me. I was very bored. And the thought of Chinelo, my girlfriend, would not leave me alone. How I loved that girl. And she didn't even know that I was in this faraway country, lonely and trashed by nostalgia, heat and dust. You never told a girl you loved that you would embark on a journey like this. That would break her heart and leave you shattered and drained before you began.

Yet the afternoon persisted in accompanying me with a headache and prickly heat. Now there was breeze and now there was none. I doused myself in water often and watched my body dry in seconds under the mango trees. From the shadows I watched the lizards lap up ants and make split-second love in the sun. I lit a cigarette, thought of a void, of space and of nothing. God, this was boredom. How long was this journey going to last?

'Cava, môn frère, môn ami,' someone said to me, coming into the compound.

Ah, that was Dr Johnson, smiling lavishly at me in the sun and carrying a plastic chair with him. He had just walked in through the gate.

'Sunbathing in the tropics, are you?' he joked.

'No, no. Far from it,' I said. This ex-mayor delighted in being witty and catching me off-guard with it. Then I noticed that he was limping.

'Anything the matter with that leg?' I asked him.

'Oui, oh yes. As a matter of fact, I twisted this ankle years ago. But every year it comes and goes. Painful though it is, it goes. I think some people call it gout or something of the sort. It is a disease of the old and the rich, they say. But I am neither old nor rich.'

My eyes flicked in disbelief as I remembered that he had been the health minister in Sierra Leone for seven years before he took up the mayoralty of Freetown from this ousted junta at war with the West African ECOMOG forces in their last stronghold in Kono district. And he read me right immediately.

'No, no,' he protested. 'Don't get me wrong there. Left to me alone, I'd choose to believe that old age isn't as pleasant as they have had it painted. I think it is rather a period in one's life when the frolics and over-indulgence of youth begin to take their toll. But this has chosen an unwilling victim anyway because it has never stopped me from whatever I am bent on doing. It's a lazy man that stays ill beyond twenty-four hours. As for me, I've been out there all morning putting my little invention into practice. I invite you in the evening to come and have a look at it.'

'And what, by God, could that be?' I asked.

'I call it a smoke plant – eighty percent locally sourced raw material. I am inviting you this evening, and let's see what you think of it, Mr Poet.'

I was flattered. He had just read my 'Seaside Palms', a poem that featured in *Okike 36*. I accepted his invitation, it being an opportunity I had wanted to get closer to him and the rest.

'You know, it's not just enough to stay alive,' he said. 'One must try to get something done, too. I hope this invention functions as expected, else what is the use of science without technology?'

I agreed with him, knowing what he meant from the earlier conversations we had had before. He insinuated of course that a man like himself, thoroughly educated, should be able to produce something tangible at a time like this, unlike his colleagues, who had pure military education and couldn't do anything else other than play draughts, chess or cards all day long. I had heard too that he had read more than one university degree, and I was enthusiastic to visit this smoke plant of his in the evening.

That same evening however, Fatoumata came home earlier than usual. She had a very luminescent face and there was spring in her step. She was visibly happy as I welcomed her into the sitting room.

'How are you, Oosy? And where is Kayode?'

'Must be somewhere outside. You didn't see him out there?'

She shook her head and let her handbag slide onto the centre stool. Oh, Fatoumata had an affectionate way of calling my name that made me want to fall in love with her. The way her lips formed as she called 'Oosy' instead of 'Osy' thrilled me to the soul. She was beautiful, soft and affectionate in her ways generally and this could be quite misleading.

'At last,' she said, 'we have been able to submit your passports for the visas. Uhh, what a relief!'

She dropped herself on the sofa and my eyes lit up.

'What!' I cried.

'Consider it done!' she announced. 'The officer assured me to expect them five weeks from today. Now Kayode can go back to Lagos to get his health back as he has wished. His mother has asked me to buy your tickets fast so you can come back when your visas are out.'

'He has been smoking all day, so I guess he's much better now.'

'Oohh, this boy wants to kill me with this his malaria pala-ver. I will check out the tickets first thing tomorrow morning,' concluded Fatoumata.

She was quite relieved. But certainly not as relieved as I was. I had helped Kayode convince his mother that it was best if he flew back home as soon as the visas were applied for. Now it had worked. And suddenly the prospects of seeing Chinelo again became real to me, too real to be believed. This was a girl who had meant everything to me. When I had left for this journey, the fear of travelling from Guinea Conakry and not seeing her again in a terribly long time ate away half of my heart. Now she seemed so near and so real that I wouldn't have minded if we left for Lagos the next day. Such was how I felt.

Kayode was very happy too when I gave him the news out-side. And he couldn't stop smoking either. He could smoke like that too when he was worried. As we went strolling from there, we took the pathway through a corn farm that was covered with dust. There were hens everywhere clucking, pecking and scratch-ing the ground. Everywhere smelled of smoke, even when you couldn't see where it came from. I remembered Dr Johnson's smoke plant and told Kayode we would be seeing him togeth-er when we came back. We took all the detours we knew round the neighbourhood until we came out onto the asphalt under construction. It was hazy toward Kipe and Ratoma. The sun was beginning to go down fast, leaving bits of orange- and pur-ple-coloured clouds lingering on the horizon. So we traced our way home fast, too, heading toward the direction of Dr Johnson's smoke plant. But he was not there yet as I had expected. So we came to the gate and looked into the corner where the president's guests, as we called them, used to sit and discuss politics. It was deserted. Quite unusual at that time of the day. The entire compound suddenly felt creepy and deserted. All the mango trees and the many flowers were still. The breeze had gone. There was no sign of even a breath of air. Everything was still.

At last we looked at one another and with buckling courage stepped into the compound. As we approached our door, the girl that kept house for Fatoumata burst out of the kitchen, startling us. Her face was hooded and solemn. Her nipples jutted out on her chest from behind a white t-shirt and her breasts bounced up and down as she came down to meet us.

'Have you heard what happened?' she cried, stopping short of pressing her chest into mine.

'What? What happened?'

'They came and took them away. All of them. The military police did. It was so hurriedly done you could sense it wasn't right at once. They just hauled them into their van and drove away. They weren't happy at all.' Her Sierra Leonian accent was obvious.

'To where?' I asked, as if I had any hand in the matter.

'Who knows?' She shrugged, waited a while and trotted back up the stairs again into the kitchen. 'They have never taken them away like this before. They have been the ones to go to the police station by themselves to sign up. Who knows if they will ever come back again?' she finally said.

I panicked. And Kayode lit another cigarette.

'Is madam Fatou in?' I asked the girl.

'No, she left soon afterwards. Madam was scared too.'

We passed the entire evening in a graveyard-like silence. Something dreadful had happened and we couldn't break away from its claws. Fatoumata came back late that night and announced that some tickets to Lagos had been found and that we would be travelling tomorrow evening. Were we excited? I wished I could tell, because everything was happening so fast. And they were all caught up in too much silence. We knew we were avoiding something, and we all connived to avoid it until the last moment. So this silence ruled over us with an iron fist until the following day when we finally boarded the flight to Lagos and escaped from its grip. But not even a momentary relief settled with us until we landed in Murtala Mohammed International Airport, Lagos, and Kayode looked at me with a dry smile and said, 'Comme ci, comme ça.'

'C'est la vie,' I said, and we headed to disembark.

***

It must have been on a Monday of the second week that followed. It was a hot morning even though the sun was nowhere to be seen. I took a bottle of cold water from the fridge and came out on the corridor upstairs to air myself. That was when the BBC news began in the sitting room. Then I heard it, the dreadful news. This was on a date I would never ever forget, the 19th October 1998…

'…In the early hours of this morning,' said the newscaster, 'we received a report confirming that Colonel Sese, the secretary to the ousted junta, and his co-plotters taken from Conakry have been publicly executed…'

I sighed again and again, and I fell into an armchair.

This meant that all the president's guests had been summarily executed. What a trial, what a ritual! What had they been traded for? Who had pawned them away in this perpetual power struggle that raged on voraciously in Africa? Lansana Conte or who? What could be worse than a presidential pawn? It simply amounted to a fate sealed to the bitter end, especially in the hands of a desperate dictator who had precariously clung to power for too long.

Now the journey back to Conakry for our visas had become an emotional one. 'Comme ci, comme ça, c'est la vie.' I could perpetually hear Colonel Nelson's voice behind those words laced with a copious smile that was truly haunting. I was yet to understand, however, how life, with only a flip of the finger, could turn instantly into a nightmare.

It was foggy and it was cold. You couldn't see anything beyond sixty metres. And when you breathed, your breath came out of your nostrils like smoke from windpipes. It was the second morning this week that we had had it this cold and foggy in Ceuta, as once again, from the Moroccan–Spanish frontier, the fog rolled down from the Jebel Musa mountain called The Dead Woman. As always, it drifted across Benzu – the border settlement – and curled its way toward the city centre, heavy in its woolly obscurity. It was about a quarter to eight, yet the world was still asleep. All you heard was the splashing of waves at the rocks and at the shingles. The Mediterranean Sea was unusually loud and restless this morning. But it did not bring with it the strong wind I had expected, only the smell of something green and decaying that brought an unpleasant taste to my mouth.

I kept very close to the right side of the road because the left side, where the road ran dangerously close to the edge of the steep shore, made me giddy. It was precarious, too, even on this side, for I had to feel my way through the fog and strain my ears for the rumbling of a truck or the chugging sound of a car. My early morning disappointment hadn't made me less cautious and neither had the eerie solitariness of this Benzu road. My disappointment at having failed to reach my fiancée by telephone, for which I had trekked from Calamocarro to Benzu, was quite tortuous. More so when this outdated Spanish telephone system by Telefonica had chopped off a chunk of money from my telephone card without allowing a single call through. Because I knew of no other way to contact her, I was upset, and I lit a cigarette and walked to the next bend where the road again crept into the seaside rocks.

Turning into this bend, I observed that I had left the thicker part of the fog behind; I could now see about a hundred metres ahead. I didn't know why, but I felt a great relief. Then I heard the loud tooting of a horn from the sea and knew that a ship or a ferry was on its way to the port. When I came to a small beach in front, I saw in the vague distance the murky shape of car parked on the untarred left side of the road. I hadn't seen it on my way to Benzu. But now there it was, so cold and immobile like metal scrap, just as if it were something that had suddenly materialised out of the milky fog. I studied it as I drew nearer and for no apparent reason, I became apprehensive. Yet I crossed over to the side of the road where the car was parked because the road had bent again, leaving me exposed to any dangerous-driving Arab teenager who might chance to meet me on the track.

I surveyed the ominously quiet surrounding for signs of whoever might have parked it but couldn't see anyone around. It could have been left by one of the men who usually came early for fishing. But there was no sign of life as far down the rock-studded beach as I could see. Perhaps whoever it was might have disappeared behind one of the many gigantic rocky protrusions with his fishing kit. But looking harder still, I saw seagulls scrounging for food at the frothing edge of the beach while they ran back and forth from the waves that kept fizzling out in feckless foam. All the time the visibility got clearer and clearer. A little tail-less brown dog ran along the coastline from the other end, stopping now and then, too, to sniff at the pebbles and at the seaweed deposits on which the gulls scavenged. As the dog closed in on them, they flew up, and settled again when it had passed. Soon I felt the heat of the cigarette in between my fingers and quickly drew the last drag and flung the butt away.

As I walked close to the car, I saw through its wound up window on the driver's seat a yellow plastic basket filled with children's nappies and some coloured pegs. A brown teddy bear lay face down on the heap of clothing with other household effects at the back of the seat. There was a yellow pair of high-heeled shoes, a big brushing comb, a plastic can, a hand dryer, a small wooden chest, a mangled bunch of table flowers and some brightly coloured clothing that covered the rest of the disorderly heap. The car, an old-model Peugeot 309, was dirty with dust and finger marks. And looking drab in its oxblood paint it appeared more frozen than forsaken, yet still it seemed as if it were on the verge of dematerialising. I hurried past it, feeling a little disconcerted. The urge to look at it once again was absolute, and I turned to reassure myself that at least it wasn't up to any vanishing trick. And that was when I saw her.

At that same moment the seagulls let out a howl into the cold air. And with wings flapping frantically they flew into the fog, still howling even when they had disappeared into the misty whiteness. The waves rolled on faster and faster against the shore, breaking into white foam as they splashed on the many rocks jutting out of the sea like stumps of rotten wood. A red car tore through the asphalt behind, in the manner of a phantom machine. Another protracted blasting of a ship's horn sailed over from the direction of Ceuta port. And with it came a lingering smell of something fresh taken from the bottom of the sea. I turned to meet her eyes.

Cold mystery shot through me from within the dimmed brown eyes that met mine. I swallowed hard as I tried to absorb the scene before me. She was lying in a sleeping bag on the ground behind the car. Her hair was long, dark and golden, with such curls that made it luxuriant and girlish. Pulling herself together, she squinted as if the white surrounding were a midday sun to her eyes. A lock of hair fell across her face and she shoved it aside. Never before had I seen freckles look so beautiful on a woman. Although her forehead was creased and her stare sad and distant, the allure of youth and agelessness radiated from within her, from beneath the dark mystery of her eyes. Suddenly I felt cold looking at her; she seemed trapped in a flood of despair. Strange that she had transmitted this through her eyes and through the freckles on her face. And I felt instantly in my blood the need to reach out to her, although I did not know how.

Should I talk to her? Would she respond? But I was a complete stranger to her world. And to think that I knew nothing of the murder or rape statistics of this small city. Did I fit into the picture frame of a murderer or a rapist? Would she scream if I opened my mouth? That too was totally possible, you know.

And then the fact that I was a black man in a city where men of my colour were only refugees holed up in an asylum camp on the top of a wooded hill. A monster of some sort driven out of the peace of his jungle! Of what help could I possibly be? What sense could I possibly make? A black man in a race-conscious society. A refugee. And at this hour of the day…

I took a quick but difficult rethink. Difficult because all this while, as I watched her, I saw a scene in my mind in which a little girl was drowning beside a boat in which I sailed. She was gulping down mouthfuls of water and looking up to me to pull her out of her distress, but I did nothing. All because I wanted her to cry 'Help!' Because I wanted to be asked, even though I knew she was too stunned for that.

'H-Hola,' I stammered, looking her in the face with a squint. She was no more than twenty-three.

'Hola,' she replied. She pouted her colourless lips and immediately slipped back into her sleeping bag like a snail.

This was the moment I had dreaded, and my feet grew heavy like logs. I despaired, not knowing whether to go or to stay. But seeing that she was in no haste to crawl out of her shell I blamed my forwardness in the matter and dragged myself away. A few metres into the fog I began to feel anew the cold that some minutes ago did not exist for me. I turned and looked back and to my surprise she was looking at me. And as our eyes met, she turned away and stared at the waves. In that solemn stare again was an unspoken despair. I stood there and watched her slip into the sleeping bag again. What the devil was wrong with her, I thought and suddenly decided that whatever it was, it was worth investigating. I stopped and pretended to watch the waves and the seagulls that were now back on the shore. For how long I stood there I could not tell. But I stood long enough until my legs began to ache. Then, suddenly, I decided that I would finally leave for the camp if she looked at me again. But as though she had picked up on my thought, she took up the challenge, lying still in those cold minutes, not stirring one bit, having apparently wiped me from her mind.

From beside the rocks I walked down to the shore, still watching from the corner of my eye to see if she would look in my direction. She did not, and I was determined to make her. I picked up a pebble and flung it at the seabirds. They howled, panicked and flew into the misted air. She did not even stir. I headed for the camp. But it was perhaps curiosity that made me look back again when I got to a bend. And I caught her at that moment turning to look at me. As I turned to go, I saw her wave her hand. Did I imagine it? She waved again and motioned me to come. And despite the distance and the fog in between, I thought I saw her teeth, as though she had smiled, only that I couldn't swear to it because of the fog.

Befogged by what to say and how to say it before I reached her, I quickly lit another cigarette to clear the haze. She sat up as I approached and reclined on the car, having unzipped the sleeping bag halfway and pulled it up with the rest of her body. I could see that she was tall.

And looking at her from so close a range now, she looked more like a runaway schoolgirl: young, defiant, stubborn and obviously deluded by something, the scope of which it wasn't in her grasp to understand. But she really was beautiful, which to my mind was a dangerous asset, even for her. Because in spite of herself, her pastoral beauty seemed the sort that would attract the type of beasts that would not transform into princes. You could see that sort of problem all over her.

'Hola,' I said.

'Hola,' she murmured, and she drew her eyes into slits and looked around her and at the sea. In silence we stood as she stared, shoving one lock of hair after another from her face and looking totally withdrawn.

At the beach below, the waves advanced in half-rings and violent tongues, and the fog seemed to rise from the surface of the sea like steam. The seagulls and other smaller birds lay in a mass far from the shingles, pruning their feathers. The fog thickened and a cold breeze hummed in my ears. And then I despaired as the solid barrier between us confronted me head on.

What language should I speak? Spanish? I had so little knowledge of it that any meaningful communication with her would be impossible and wouldn't lead anywhere except into farce. And there was nothing about the situation I faced that allowed for the comical. It was unimaginable that I hadn't thought about this earlier. I felt thoroughly trapped.

There was silence. What could possibly be going on in her mind, I wondered, while minutes dragged on lazily as if they were hours.

'Est-ce que tu parles français ou anglais?' she asked.

Bubbles escaped from my chest; the feeling of being able to communicate was beyond freedom.

'Anglais,' I said quickly, 'English and a little French.'

She licked her lips and looked at me through the slits of her eyes.

Cocking her head, she said, 'Well, you're one of the pretenders of this world, aren't you?'

Her words were like an early morning slap across my face.

'I don't understand,' I said, forcing a smile. 'What is it exactly you mean?'

'You were supposed to be minding your business along that road. How come you came down looking at the drab shore and the seabirds? You haven't seen seagulls before?' she asked.

'I didn't stop to look just at the seagulls,' I said.

'Then at what?'

'At virtually everything: the waves, the birds… and examining my thoughts .'

'At everything,' she smiled, 'and that includes me, eh?''

'You're right.'

'You're smart, aren't you? Just like my husband, thinking and believing he can get away with everything.' There was a sour note in her voice that frightened me. 'Men, hmmm.' She grinned. 'How long have you been here in Ceuta?'

'Six weeks, I suppose.'

'In Calamocarro?'

'Yes,' I answered, feeling a chill in my heart, because in Ceuta, Calamocarro meant REFUGEES. THE UNWANTED. THE UNINTELLIGENT. THE UNCOUTH. AVOID. AVOID.

She took a sharp look at my legs and, probably sensing that she had touched a sore point, changed the subject.

'Well, I think you didn't just stop to look at the shore and to examine your thoughts.'

'You're right.'

'Oh yeah?' she said. 'So aren't you a great pretender then?' Even with the greatness she had affixed to it, the word 'pretender' wasn't attractive to me, and I wondered why she felt I should get on well with it.

'To pretend and to be a pretender are not exactly the same thing, you know,' I said, willing to go wherever this discourse might lead.

'So what's the difference?' She cocked her head like a high-school girl. It was obvious to me that she wasn't really interested in the difference, if ever there was any, but I went ahead to explain all the same.

'To be a pretender could be a lifelong thing, a way of life, while to pretend could be such a casual thing, you know, a once-in-a-while situation. The former has depth; the latter hasn't.'

'Oh yeah? You're smart, aren't you? Just like my husband, having it off right now on the side and pretending it is a casual affair. I hate that word "casual". It hurts so much, so much. It hurts more than the "serious"; it's deeper than any depth.'

She suddenly went cold and pale on the cheeks and a wild creature stared from the slits of her eyes. Her legs wiggled inside the sleeping bag and she knotted her hands into fists against her shins. But for the colour of life on her face and hands, she looked like a classical statue in marble. This, too, was a danger-ous asset to her and perhaps to any man close to her heart. For no sooner had I thought this than she fixed a sphinx smile on her face and turned to me.

'Why are men like that, eh? You like them so much and yet you still desire so fanatically to murder them, to crush them be-cause they don't take you seriously, because they are so "casual" about everything except money and power.' She stopped abrupt-ly and bit her lip, took a long breath and smiled wryly. 'Well, I'm sorry; this isn't your problem. We should be talking about the sea and the waves and the fog and...' She yawned, and steam rushed out of her mouth.

'No. Go on,' I said. 'I'm listening to you.'

She went silent, almost breathless. I could hear trucks and cars zoom past the asphalt behind us, their tyres screeching dryly. The breeze was still cold and that peculiar smell of the sea lingered about, damp and pungent. She wriggled her legs inside the sleeping bag again as if something discomforted her. Then taking hold of the side zip, she pulled it straight down until it stopped at her ankles. She shoved the hair off her face and stood up, at the same time drawing out a jack knife from nowhere that I could imagine. She didn't threaten me with it. She just held it as if it were some wooden plaything. But I caught the fear in the brief flash of its blade. She turned and looked me in the eyes – face to face, height to height – her pearl-like brown eyes burning into the core of my heart.

Her eyes aflame with surprise she said, 'You're listening to me?'

'Yes, go on. I'm listening,' I said, confident like a high-school teacher.

'Do you know I could kiss you for that?' she whispered.

Silence.

I felt like a prey as she fixed her eyes on mine. My breath ceased. Her lower lip dropped and golden glows welled up deep in her eyes. The world stood still, so frighteningly still. Then she flicked her eyelids and the glow vanished.

'Take,' she said.

I took the jack knife from her, and her fingers were quite cold.

'I promised myself that if I ever found just one man that could listen to me, then I wouldn't do it,' she said.

'Do what?'

'Then I wouldn't kill him, my husband, I mean.' The way she said it and quickly gathered the sleeping bag, opened the car door, flung it in and went straight for the driver's seat showed she didn't know how much she had frightened me. I still clung to the jack knife as she turned the key and brought the engine to life. I had never witnessed any encounter so impulsive.

'Muchas gracias. Ooh, thank you very much, adios,' she said and steered the car vigorously, waving her hand at me through the window. As she turned toward the asphalt I began to panic for no apparent reason.

'Hola,' I shouted after her. 'So what's your name?'

'Alicia.'

Then she pushed down hard on the throttle and zoomed off into the white mist. She could as well have been a ghost.

Five days after, as I glanced through a story on the back page of *La Luna*, I remembered that classical freckled face again. It was a story about a young woman who a night ago had so brutally and fatally stabbed her husband. How could she have gone ahead and done it? I cried, my head teeming with suggestive images. Then my hands trembled as I traced the name of the culprit from the print. Her name was Alicia Hierro. Was she by any chance the young lady by the beach?

In the night train

Mendez Alvaro station was not as crowded as Anene had expected. But he didn't think much of it as he looked at his watch every now and then. Then he lit a cigarette and walked about the platform, muttering to himself and blowing smoke in all directions. He was waiting for the last train. If he didn't get to Aluche station soon enough, he would have to wait there for the hourly bus. The few coins that jingled in his purse wouldn't take him farther than Zarzaquemada in Leganes. And on a weekend like this, to flag down a taxi in Madrid was nothing short of wilful liquidation, the economics of which he understood too well in relation to his salary. So, Anene let the cigarettes bear the rage of his agitation while he worked himself up the more.

Then he looked up through the chrome eaves of the platform. It was a dark, blank void. He couldn't see the warm night sky over Madrid. Or the unobtrusive and serene masses of pale clouds that sailed like monstrous camels, silently, towards the horizon. Or the ebullient moon that shone in splendour above all these. He was well over twenty metres underground in Mendez Alvaro. He tried to listen to a classical tune that spilled out from a small loudspeaker overhead. It was no use, because it was the grunts and groanings of the climatising machinery inside the train tunnels that he heard. Then he heard the distant chugging of a train.

When at last the train appeared through the tunnel, he saw that he had been waiting all this while at the metro section. God, what is wrong with me, he muttered to himself. What is wrong with me tonight? He cursed himself roundly and rushed for the mobile stairs to the train section. Luckily enough, a train was about to depart, and he jumped into the second coach and sat down, his heart beating like the tom tom of a macabre ritual. Even after he had closed his eyes and drawn a deep breath, a certain fogginess still lingered in his head as the train jerked and shot off noisily on its heavy metal tracks towards Atocha Correspondencia.

Seconds slithered away before he heard the slamming of a door and the ruffling of papers. He opened his eyes. Before him was standing the ticket checker with a booklet and a puncher.

'Buenas tardes. Los billetes, por favor,' the man said. Anene searched the pockets of his jacket, found the ticket and gave it to the checker, who promptly punched a triangular hole in it and gave it back. And to Anene's surprise, the checker did not tarry nor look around but went straight for the door to the next coach and disappeared behind it.

'Bloody racists,' Anene muttered. 'The pig wouldn't bother nobody else!' His African blood simmering inside him, he looked about him, sneering. He wondered too if anyone saw the clouded spite on his face. But seeing that the coach was virtually empty, he regretted his outburst. Except for the couple that sat two seats away on his left, and a woman that sat like a collapsible needlework on the last seat to the end of the coach, the entire coach was empty. What he had thought were fellow passengers were merely the headrests of seats seen through the corner of his eye. He shook his head, blamed his general nervousness and quickly pushed the thought out of his mind.

But another thing immediately caught his attention. A little way away from where he sat was a couple sitting so intimately close, so close that they seemed cramped into one seat together. But it wasn't this amorous posture that piqued his curiosity. What struck Anene was their sharp physical contrast. He had not seen in years a couple this remarkably odd. They were such a couple that would make one remain forever puzzled as to why some relationships were so illogical and curious, bordering oftentimes on absurdity. For Anene, it was like getting trapped in the labyrinth of a puzzle. Looking at the girl, what sprang up in his mind's eye, mysterious as it was, was the livid image of a plump rose being choked by crooked brambles. The girl gave you that impression at a sudden glance, even afterwards. Her presence was breath-taking, and she was beautiful. Profoundly beautiful, Anene thought. Wasn't she like a master's painting? Or like classical prose? Perhaps more like a sonnet. And thinking of a sonnet, all at once Shakespeare's 'Shall I compare thee to a summer's day?' surged into his mind. He remembered vividly, too, Emile Zola's apt description in *The Maid of the Dawber*: 'Is she beautiful? You could not analyse her features or determine the contours of her face. She intoxicates you at first sight, as strong wine does on the first glass. All you see is a whiteness amidst a red flame, a rosy smile… She turns your head and you are already too captivated to study her perfections one by one.' Her facial charms were such that made one who knew a thing or two about arts search for classical models. And because Anene knew about the arts and because he had the time, he insisted on analysing her features; moreover, since the couple were so absorbed in each other, they provided no counter- stare to his own.

So from where he sat, Anene stared at the side of the girl's face. And when she rummaged in her handbag for something, he saw it all – all her beauty – and his heartbeat quickened. She had long, glossy black hair that rolled down her shoulders. Her hair was full, and it shimmered in the soft light whenever she moved her head. Her brows were a thin pencil line like Da Vinci's measured strokes. Her nose was straight and narrow and had such thrilling curves at the sides of its tip that were it the craft of a mortal sculptor it would have been impossible to imagine the strain and sweat of chisel work that had gone into its perfection. Her cheeks were smooth and spotless, while her lips, glistening under a deep-red lipstick, looked so luscious that any man who looked on them would think of strawberries dipped in honey. Yet nothing compared to her eyes! They were soft and translucent blue as the coastline of a tranquil sea, while their gem-like pupils were emerald green, dark at the core like tropical vegetation. In these eyes was a veritable union of the colours of life – the sea and vegetation. But what charmed Anene most was that her face, on the whole, had something indefinite and inscrutable, something of a Mona Lisa – a spectre of mystery and cold curiosity. You couldn't tell with certainty if her mind was fixed on a lofty philosophical thought, or if she were merely on the verge of breaking into a most delicate smile. Such was her charm!

More charming yet was the simplicity of her dress. She wore a long black coat and a tight-fitting long skirt. Inside the coat was a sky-blue turtleneck that no doubt concealed the ringed delight of her lovely neck. Except for a slim necklace on her neck and a small gold ring on her small finger, she wore no other jewellery, not even earrings. She appeared love-struck, pampered and over-cuddled, with an elusive presence that could conjure up what was or was not. She seemed the sort of girl that brought to your nose the delicate perfumes of exotic flowers even when they were not there. The colour and texture of her skin suggested that she probably grew up on the sunny coast of Spain and in her later years spent her time in cool, airconditioned places. You could see, too, that she wasn't made for rough and hard things, having probably been nurtured on such delicacies as skimmed milk, yoghurt, chocolate and fruit juice. She appeared that delicate.

But the man on whom she doted was anything but delicate. He was lean. He was wiry. He was tall. All these attributes stood apart, unified only by an inflammable disposition which he exuded. He was all bones, hard crystallised bones that didn't seem capable of wearing out even in the roughest of weather. His seemingly gentle and choreographed manners notwithstanding, or the Mephistophelian aura in which he basked, he certainly looked violent. His hair was black, oiled, neatly cut and combed backwards. And this deliberately exaggerated his veined and receding forehead. His eyes were dark and mysterious and gave Anene the creepy feeling, as they met his own, that he had stared down a deep disused well. His hawkish nose, long and narrow, must have determined the meagre lips and the sharp jaw that in some comical way made him look like a genius of some sort. But he didn't look like the kind of genius for better things. Yet, Anene felt that this man was in control of his life, as well as the life of this beauty, who obviously depended entirely on him. His age? It was difficult to tell, although Anene felt that fifty was safe enough for a guess. But the girl by his side was no more than twenty-four.

While Anene still studied this pair of strange lovers, the ticket checker came back, solemn and fatigued, and proceeded toward the engine cabin. The couple began again to kiss and fondle like teenagers. Anene felt the heat of their passion spreading across the empty coach in steamy breaths and muffled groans. Suddenly the man shoved his overcoat on the seat beside him, pulled the girl on his lap and with his hand in her luxuriant hair he began to suck on her lollipop lips. And with lustier passion, the girl wriggled all over him, breathing rapidly.

Suddenly, a sizzling hush fell over the entire coach like a long-drawn sigh. Anene's ears buzzed. The trundling sound of the train on the rails seemed far and faint. He felt a sudden sharp drop in the warmth and the brilliance of the lighting. The coach swerved uncomfortably left as if negotiating a bend.

Anene could tell from the tinted windows that the train had just rammed into a tunnel because an interminable row of lights now ran on both sides like thin yellow streams. Then a recorded feminine voice broke out from the unseen speakers overhead: 'Proxima parada, Atocha Correspondencia con linea uno de metro...' The train began to reduce speed. The lights came on full again and with them came the crunch and grind of heavy metal on rail tracks. The train ground to a halt. Because of its location, its train and metro lines, Puerta de Atocha station was the second busiest in Madrid after Chamartin. There was hardly any doubt in his mind that nearly all the seats would be taken. Anene felt uncomfortable, knowing that a lot of people would crowd into the coach and interrupt the live show he was watching.

He was wrong. Although there were lots of people on the platform when he looked through the window, they soon disappeared into the other coaches or didn't get on board at all. Three men and a woman who got into his own coach quickly left for the next coach. Anene swiftly reasoned that most people often neglected the first set of coaches. But in his heart, it was gladdening to remain the sole audience of a passionate act. Fortunately, the enamoured couple were not distracted by the eventual departing of the train. They went on kissing as before while the train rammed its way at a shuddering speed towards Embajadores.

For the first time, Anene felt a sudden warmth in his groin and a worm-like stirring, which triggered an unwanted erection. He crossed his legs and turned away, looking at the red neon signs overhead that told the time, the temperature and the next destination.

When he turned his attention toward the couple again, he saw that the Mephistophelian gentleman was now relaxed and less engaged. His face was flushed, and a network of veins ran like cables across his neck and forehead. His eyes were closed and his breath deep and long drawn. Lifeless as a statue, he held the girl with one hand across her shoulder while the other hand lay on his lap. And now, holding him tight, the girl busied herself kissing him hard on the side of his neck. Anene could tell how hard from the occasional twitches of facial muscles rippling through the man's reddening face. Then suddenly the man stiffened and grew pale. His eyelids tightened and flickered convulsively. His bony, slender arms tightened around his lover's shoulders. He winced, gasped and made the short and sharp exhaling sounds of one who is climaxing. The girl still clung to his neck, kissing him, while her mass of luxuriant hair heaved lustfully in the soft light. Then gradually the man's grip on her shoulders slackened and he began to fondle her neck. She purred like a kitten and began slowly to withdraw her face from his neck. As she withdrew, Anene saw on the side of the man's neck, by a dilated vein, a trickle of blood which, clashing with the coach light, gleamed like a red gem.

Anene's eyes became transfixed and his heartbeat stopped.

As the man slowly opened his eyes and met Anene's cold stare, he turned away and felt his neck with one hand and looked at it. Seeing the blood, he turned the girl's mouth to his neck again. And in the next icy moments that followed, the girl sucked the blood dry, kissed the man on the mouth and pressed her finger on the lacerated point on his neck. Anene shook his head to stabilise his senses while the train swung to the left with a thin grating noise. This often happened on the stiff bend between Atocha and Embajadores stations. But this night the noise took on a clear, horrid tone as if the train had lost control and was hurtling into the bowels of the earth. A thrill ran through Anene's spine. He held onto the cold chrome sidebar of his seat to steady himself.

Looking up later, he saw that monstrous beauty of a girl turn her rose- tinted face deliberately. It was so obvious it was deliberate – she turned her face toward him. And in the sudden flash of eyes, his eyes caught her eyes and – Lord of Hosts! – he saw that the colours of life had vanished from her eyes. Now boring deep like drills into his own eyes was the most diabolical glare of the age of horror, corruption and despicable vices. It was like looking into a pit of immortal hatred and eternal ruins.

Anene's head swelled and he shuddered. It was all too revolting.

In a sudden bolt, he got onto his legs and scampered toward the door of the next coach, muttering, 'Damned, damned.' He observed, even in his hurry, that the illusive perfume of warmth and passion that had once filled the coach had given way to a cold odour of something corrupt and nauseous. And the seat where the old woman had sat by herself like a collapsible needlework now had a human-sized bat-like creature on it, grinning at his predicament.

The author

Osita Obi was born in Onitsha, Nigeria in 1962 and has a BA (Hons) degree in English. He lives in Manchester, is married and has two children. Since graduating from university, Osita's passion has been writing poetry and prose. His work has appeared in numerous anthologies and journals, including Okike, Revue Noire, Farafina Online, Sonnie Adegboyin's Frontiers: Nigerian Short Stories and Helon Kabila and Kadija Sesay's Dreams, Miracles and Jazz: New Adventures in African Writing. Osita's own published works include The Girl Who Loved the Wind and Other Stories and a novel, Rage of the Sea Lion-one of five nominated for Association of Nigerian Authors (ANA) award for prose 2020. His latest work, The Monster Comes to Ceuta and Other Migrant Stories, is a product of his four-month stay at Calamocarro, a refugee camp in Ceuta, Spain.